A Boy of Two Worlds

A Boy of Two Worlds

Lorna Eglin

Christian Focus Publications

Dedicated, with love, to

Georgie Orme,

the real 'Naado' of this story

who has given 25 years of

her life, to helping and loving

a multitude of the Disabled

Children of Kenya.

Contents

Meet your new Friend, Lemayan.

Lemayan is the special friend that you will meet and get to love as you read this story. He lives in a Maasai village on the vast plains of southern Kenya. Not a village as you know it, but a large circle of dry thorn branches forming a fence, with ten or more family homes scattered inside the circle. The houses are shaped like loaves of bread, or rather like a circle of elephants sitting down! All the rest of the space in the enclosure is for the cattle, sheep and goats that the Maasai people delight in.

The cattle give them milk – the food they like best - for breakfast, lunch and supper! The sheep and goats provide a good feast of meat, but by no means every day. The sheep and goats are their 'money' that they can exchange for other necessities, such as tobacco for the men, tea and sugar for the grannies, chewing gum for the children, and, for the mothers, more important things like soap to keep their children clean, red dye for the various cloths they wear and sometimes, in times of drought, foreign food like potatoes, maize meal, and dry maize and beans.

Lemayan's greatest love is the herd of cattle his father owns. Cattle are the pride of the Maasai people, their reason for living. Lemayan loves that life and hopes never to leave it. But in our story something happens to him that takes him out of his familiar world, to another world of school, hospitals, strange towns and even a big city. There are many struggles in his heart about which world to follow, which road to take. In all the battles his heart goes out to the Good Shepherd,

Jesus and when he finally comes to follow Him with all his heart, the two worlds come together.

The name Lemayan means 'blessing'. He certainly had many blessings in his young life, but as he grew up he became a blessing to many people, as he brought the old ways of the Maasai and the new ways of our western world together. They found out that 'Enkai', the Creator, whom they had always revered, had a Son, Jesus, whom He had sent to be the Saviour of all people – the old and the new.

So, read on, enjoy your friend Lemayan's life and adventures with him, and, like him be blessed in following Jesus who is your Good Shepherd also.

Lemayan's Safe, Warm World

'Help! Lemayan! Come here quickly! Come and hold this lamb for me,' an old woman called to her grandson urgently. Lemayan rushed to her rescue, snatched up the wriggling lamb and cuddled it in his arms, feeling very important, while his granny triumphantly filled her mug with frothy milk from the mother of the lamb. The trouble had been that the lamb and granny had been competing for milk from the same ewe at the same time!

It was 'the time of the buffalo,' as the Maasai call that part of the early morning when the first light of dawn streaks the sky. Life was beginning to wake in the homestead as people emerged one by one from their low houses, and the cattle, goats and sheep stirred in their thorn-branch enclosures.

Earlier, Lemayan had slithered off the cow-skin that was the communal bed for the small children of the family, fumbled for his stick and hurried outside. The stick was important. It was his identity. Girls never carried sticks. But all boys had them because they were the herders, those who cared for the livestock. Girls helped their mothers with the milking. They had their uses. But he was a boy. Small as he was, he must be careful always to carry his stick, even though he had as yet no use for it. He shivered and pulled the crumpled cloth, his scanty clothing, tighter around him. Inside the house it was still dark and quiet and stuffy-warm, but outside the air was fresh and a new day was about to start.

He had stood quietly, hugging himself in the cold, as he watched his mother bend, gourd in hand, to milk the first cow of this morning. That done, she straightened up and solemnly poured a little milk into the pointed skin cap that was the lid of the gourd. All the girls out to help with the morning milking, paused to watch her. She splashed the milk in the lid, up towards the sky and prayed. Looking up at the morning star she called out in a clear voice:

You, who rises yonder, I pray to you, hear me.

Keep my cattle safe. Take care of our people.

 Bless this home.

Then the milking began in earnest. The smaller girls held back the calves, lambs and kids, so that the big girls and mothers could quickly fill the milk gourds before the desperate baby animals had their share.

Five years old now, Lemayan was awakening to the magic of the early mornings when the animals started stirring and the big folk began the daily bustle. Everyone had a job. Everyone except him! They said he was too small. Everyone else knew exactly what to do, what his place in the life of the village was. But he just darted around, getting in everyone's way, hoping they'd include him somehow in the busyness.

Now, with granny's summons, Lemayan's heart swelled with pride. He was needed! He had a job! He had a part in the care of these beautiful animals. She had trusted him! She had needed him to help her! He held the soft, silky squirming lamb firmly, but oh, so gently. He poured all the love of his little heart into that warm, fragrant scrap of life. Having finished taking her share of the milk from the ewe, his granny called to Lemayan to release the lamb, which then scampered away to its breakfast on wobbly legs. Lemayan gazed with pride at this greedy lamb - tail flicking, head butting its mother to ensure a good flow of milk. Satisfied, the lamb staggered off and Lemayan strolled about trying to get in the way of another job.

On that day his love for the home animals was born - cattle, goats and sheep, the pride of all true Maasai. He loved the sight, the feel and the smell of the cattle, and even of the goats. That smell was home, security and the whole of his life – he was a Maasai! He was a boy! One day he would be an 'olmorani,' one of those proud handsome glorious warriors, lords of creation! His cup was full. His name meant 'blessing' and truly he was a blessed one!

As the months went on he was given more and more jobs to match his eagerness. Other boys of his age were content to play around but Lemayan was happiest when sharing in a small way, the work with the cattle. He delighted in identifying the calf of a cow being milked, then quickly leading it to get its share of the milk from two teats while the woman stripped the other two. His mother wanted milk for the family but he knew that father was proud of his eager son who, so young, had recognised the supreme importance of the calves – the future of their herd.

'Lemayan lai,' his father called to him one wonderful day, 'drive these calves outside and tether them in the shade of the 'oltepesi' - a nearby acacia tree. Lemayan nearly burst with importance. His father had asked him, him alone, without a bigger boy to take the credit. He drove the calves proudly, making all the whistling, encouraging noises required to keep them together, and tethered them in the shade to rest. His little fingers knotted the stiff rawhide straps carefully just as he had seen his elders do. The calves were happy, their tummies satisfied. Their mothers would go far off to graze but the calves had to await their return.

When the calves were safely tied up, then came playtime. Sometimes they played 'raiding'. Each boy had a number of marked stones as his 'cattle'. Which they tried to steal from each other, while still faithfully protecting their own. They dreamed

of the future when they would be warriors and go on glorious raids on the other tribes and drive home the booty. Lemayan, usually the youngest of the herders, lost most of his 'cattle'.

But when they played 'riddles' Lemayan often shone. He was a clever boy and when once he had heard a riddle he remembered it. He gained the respect of bigger boys as quite often he caught them out with riddles they couldn't answer but he seldom got caught out himself. This game became uproarious as they laughed at each other's attempts at answers, at the double meaning of the riddle and at the hidden humour.

'Life is good,' thought Lemayan. 'It must go on like this for ever.' Herding, playing, learning, growing – preparing for the life of a warrior, and eventually an elder, a respected man of his tribe.

'Father, please don't ever send me away to school,' asked Lemayan one day. 'I want to stay with you, and with our cattle always.' Thus he voiced his greatest fear to his father. Now six years old, he had recently lost the first of his baby teeth – the age when some boys were sent far away to school, into another life.

'My son,' his father smiled at him reassuringly, 'I will certainly not waste such a good herdsman as you on school. Let lazy boys go to school, disobedient boys, crippled ones or stupid. I'll keep you with me. You are skilled and precious to me.' So he built up a reputation for himself as a true Maasai, one who loved and valued what God had given to his people. He would never be sent to school. When the chief was required by the government to fill his quota of boys for school, he would always be overlooked. He was safe!

A Glimpse of other Worlds

'I am driving two steers to sell at the cattle auction next week,' Father announced one day. 'You, Lemayan, and your bigger brother, will come with me to the stock-sale driving four goats. There has been little rain this season. Soon we will need money to buy maize-meal and other foodstuffs, as the milk will not be enough. We also need money to buy another donkey. If the rains fail completely, we will have to move and we will not have enough donkeys to carry our loads.'

The thought of possible famine didn't mean much to Lemayan. To him, life was a glorious round of herding, milking and drinking milk in abundance. But he rejoiced to be with his father, to help with the animals. He looked forward to seeing Land Rovers and lorries. Things he had heard of from boys who had ventured out to trading centres or cattle auction sales but now he would see them for himself.

Lemayan had a long drink of milk before he emerged from the warm hut on the great day of the journey. Father and bigger brother, already out in the misty half-light of the early morning, had caught the animals that were to be sold, from the rest of the still sleepy herds. Lemayan hurried in to keep them cornered, whistling and waving his arms, while his brother tied skin straps round

17

their necks. Then they all set off, with goodbye waves from the women and girls who by that time were busy with the milking.

The three of them had a hard time at first. The six animals they were driving were determined to turn back home. Agile Lemayan was in his element, running this way and that, fielding the bewildered animals. Gradually they all settled down to an easy and steady walk across the vast plain. The cattle-sale was held far behind the hills in the distance. When their path joined a wide dirt road, they felt they were getting nearer.

'What's that?' Lemayan cried out in fright. There was a loud roar behind him and it was getting louder by the minute. They all turned round and saw a huge cloud of dust approaching.

'Quick!' exclaimed Father, 'It's a lorry coming! Catch the animals.' They were nearly too late. The terrified animals were panicking, running off in different directions. Then Lemayan understood why they had tied the rawhide straps round their necks in the morning before they left home. Without them it would have been hard to catch and hold those frightened animals. The lorry passed while Lemayan held on with all his young strength to the two goats in his charge. The dust around them settled and the livestock calmed down. Only when it was all over did Lemayan realise that he had not really seen the lorry. He had certainly heard it, he had been enveloped in its dust, but he was still to see the thing called a lorry.

But the lorry was not the only thing of wonder to see at the cattle sale. Yes, there were lorries and Land Rovers but also tractors with trailers and even a bus. For the first time in his life he neglected his duties with his beloved animals and rushed around to see one wonder after another, till hunger drove him to look for Father and his brother. Father understood both his excitement and his hunger and gave him a big, square, greasy 'mandasi' (doughnut) to eat, and didn't even scold him.

The 'munanda', or stock-sale, teemed with the familiar red-blanketed Maasai elders sitting in the shade, 'eating the news' with men from other areas, and handsome warriors striding about, proudly tossing their long pigtails, well smeared with red-ochre and sheep's fat.

But there were other strange people about. Women in brightly coloured dresses and headscarves, sitting selling cabbages, oranges, sweet potatoes and tobacco. One woman had a charcoal fire and was roasting juicy green maize-cobs. Father bought one for each of his sons, but not for himself. Elders do not walk around eating in public.

There were also men in long trousers, shirts and shiny shoes. These people, so he was told, were from towns, looking for young steers to slaughter for their butcher shops. Father explained to Lemayan that those men and the women selling vegetables were of the neighbouring Kikuyu people, hardworking, good at trading, bargaining and getting rich, and very keen on putting all their children in school for as many years as possible. Lemayan felt very sorry for Kikuyu children.

There were also little short, shy men, a bit shabby, selling large paraffin-tins full of unrefined honey from their hives, far up in the highland forests. Those were the Dorobo, Father explained, from whom the Maasai bought the honey-brew to drink at weddings or any big celebrations.

Lemayan had much to tell his friends when at last they arrived home, driving the newly bought donkey, which was loaded down with Father's purchases There were gifts for everyone; tobacco for the old people to chew, a new teapot and two more mugs for Mother and new cloths for all his children, plus the dye to make them the familiar dull pinkish-red everyone wore.

One evening, in the firelight, snuggled up against Father's blanket, he asked him about these strangers, the non-Maasai whom he had seen at the munanda - people who wore unfamiliar clothes and spoke other languages.

'Father, those people, the Dorobo and Kikuyu that we saw, where do they live? What do they do? Did Enkai make them also, as he made all of us?' Lemayan, like all Maasai children, knew about Enkai, God, the great One in the heavens, who created the Maasai people.

'Yes, my son, Enkai made everything and everyone. He made people, animals, the trees and the hills, even the sun and the moon.' The other children gathered round because Father, they knew, was a good storyteller and they sensed a story was coming.

'Etii apa...' (Once upon a time there was,) Father started, and all the listeners made the required grunt to assure the storyteller that they were listening eagerly.

'Once upon a time, when Leeyio, the first man born to Naiterukop, the beginner of the world, was getting old, he called his sons to bless them and to divide their inheritance among them.' Father

20

paused and his young audience gave the awaited grunt.

'The eldest son greedily gloating at having first choice,' Father continued, 'stated his requests. He asked for land, much land to cultivate. He asked for seeds to plant, to grow many kinds of food, for the riches and prosperity that the crops would bring.

'Leeyio despised his eldest son for his greed and gave him a curved stick with which to scratch the surface of the soil to grow his vegetables. He became the father of the Kikuyu and all the peoples who make a living by scratching in the ground like chickens.' The Maasai consider the ground a sacred resource not to be dug, as it is the 'mother' of the grass their herds need for life.

'The second son was lazy. He wasn't interested in the work that scratching in the ground entailed. He eagerly pounced on a much easier life. 'Honoured Father, grant to me the forest, all the animals of the forest to hunt and the berries of the forest for food, and the honey of the forest for brewing the honey-beer that will make me happy.'

'Again, disgusted by the greed and laziness of his son, he scornfully gave him a bow and arrow. So the second son became the father of all the Dorobo who live deep in the forests of the highlands, who hunt, who gather and are skilful in harvesting honey according to the trees that flower at different seasons and varying altitudes, who supply the Maasai with their strong honey-beer.

'The third son, Maasinta, the last-born, loved his aging father deeply. Overcome by the thought of the soon-to-come sleep of his honoured father, he cried out humbly, 'Give me but your flywhisk,

your zebra-tail flywhisk, to remember you by.'
Leeyio, pleased by his humility and love, gave
him the requested flywhisk. And thus he became
the father of all Maasai.

Enkai, the great God of the skies, was so
pleased with Maasinta, with the respect he had
shown his father and with his lack of greed, that
the Maasai became his favourites, the ones he
loved and delighted in and blessed above all
others. And we are still His favourites to this day,'
he concluded.

'But what about the cattle?' the boys prompted
the storyteller, knowing that the most exciting
part of the story was still to come.

'Yes,' Lemayan's father continued, 'Enkai
decided to bless the Maasai, and them only, with
his greatest blessing. One day he called Maasinta.
'Go,' Enkai ordered, 'cut many thorn branches and
build a huge enclosure round your hut.' Maasinta
hurried off to do what Enkai had commanded.

"Tomorrow, early in the morning,' Enkai again
addressed his favourite, 'I will give you something
called cattle, my cattle, that come from heaven
itself. While they are coming, keep very silent.
Whatever you see or hear, show no sign of surprise
or fear. Make no sound at all.'

'At the 'time of the buffalo' Maasinta came to
stand in front of his house to see what would
happen, to wait for the thing that was to be
given him by Enkai himself. Presently he heard
the sound of thunder and Enkai released a wide
strong leather thong that reached from heaven
to earth. Soon cattle started descending down
the strap into the enclosure. The ground shook
with the thundering of their hooves. Maasinta

shook too in fear and wonder, but he did not make any sound or movement, just as Enkai had commanded.

'Then tragedy struck! Dorobo, who had come to visit Maasinta, bringing him his much-loved honey-beer, came rushing out of the house to see what was happening. Hearing the noise and seeing the cattle thundering down the strap, he let out a loud cry, 'Aiyiayia!' – a cry of horror and fear. But the deed was done! The cattle-flow stopped, and the strap was taken back into heaven.

' Then Enkai, thinking that it was Maasinta who had shouted, said, 'Why did you cause me to stop you giving you cattle? Did you think those were enough? Now I will never again send my cattle to earth. Care for them. Love them as I love you.'

'And that is why we Maasai love our cattle. Why we love Enkai who gave them to us. Why we take back cattle from other races, which may have some. They are really ours.

'That is of course why we hate and despise the Dorobo for cutting off the stream of the animals descending, before the world was filled with all of heaven's cattle. Now it is truly finished,' he concluded, referring to his story.

As young Lemayan snuggled down on the cow skin bed, with the other small children, he had a warm glow in his heart. 'Ashe Enkai,' (Thank you God) he whispered, the first prayer of his young heart. 'Thank you that I belong to your favourite race. Thank you for your very best gift in the whole wide world, our precious cattle. I will care for them with all my strength, all my life.' He went to sleep, safe and content. But his life was soon to be overturned.

Big Changes

The rains had failed, milk was scarce and Lemayan had to eat the food that he hated. The thick maize-meal mush his mother cooked for the family was bearable if there was a good mug of milk to wash it down, or better still, if there was a tasty bowl of goat meat and gravy. But the little milk the cows could still give, the calves drank, as they were the herd of the future. The goats were for selling, to get money to buy food – maize-meal, potatoes and horrible things called cabbages. These cabbages, Lemayan could easily see, were green leaves. Goats' food! Only goats ate leaves, not people. Mother even spoilt the cabbages for the goats because she cooked them!

Just occasionally, because it was drought and people were getting thin and weak, they had real Maasai food – blood. Lemayan watched with eager interest as three men drove a young steer into the enclosure. They tied a rawhide strap firmly round the neck of the unsuspecting animal. Then two of them held the animal still, while a third stood in readiness, with a large gourd, and a handful of fresh cow-dung and green grass.

But Lemayan's eyes were on the fourth warrior kneeling on one knee about two yards away. He had a bow and arrow and was carefully taking aim, targeting the now swollen vein in the young cow's neck. With a click the arrow flew, piercing the neck, but making just a shallow knick, as the arrow was blocked behind the point. The warrior standing by plucked the arrow out, and held the gourd to catch the bright blood that came spurting out. When the required amount was caught, he slapped a dung/grass plaster on the little wound, untied the strap, and the bewildered animal wandered off, none the worse for what had been done to it. Drinking a mug of blood made one feel really satisfied and strong. That was good food indeed!

But the cattle were getting too weak to be bled often. There was no tender grass to wean the calves. The elders gathered to talk far into the night to decide how to save both their families and their precious cattle.

'We'll have to move! The whole village must move and we must go soon!' Lemayan's father, as headman of the village, announced gravely one fateful day. 'Our warriors, our sons with whom we entrusted most of our cattle, have sent good reports. They say that on the Kaputiei Plains, near the city of Enkare Nairobi (Cold Water) the rains were fair. Our herds there are in good condition. But the cows we kept here have dried up and will soon die if we don't move them. So, unless it rains in the next few days, we will leave in four days time.'

The children were excited. Something new was happening, something that they would be involved in. The women were a bit dismayed at all the work entailed in a move – getting ready for going, packing the donkeys, the days of walking and camping out. The huge job of building new huts for their families when they arrived was women's work. But everyone agreed that the move was necessary. Cattle-people must follow the grazing, for those cattle were their life.

Some young men were sent immediately to spy out friendly villages where they could camp along the way. Walking, hindered by old folk and weak livestock, they would take at least three walking days on the journey. The men came back to report their findings. They came with a surprise that no one had expected.

'The route we have planned follows the road to Nairobi,' they explained. ' We can put our old people, and some mothers with little ones, on a bus.'

This was such a new idea that it needed much discussion. It always was a problem to know what to do about the elderly when it became necessary to move the whole community.

'I'd rather die here than go in one of those things I have only heard of!' was the vehement reply, when the news was broken to Lemayan's great-grandfather, a withered patriarch, highly honoured for his age. He was reputedly the only member still living, of his generation or age-grade - worthy of respect indeed!

'Kaguyia le Papa, (Dad's Granddad) I'll go with you and look after you!' Lemayan cried out in love for the old man. Later, after the elders accepted his offer, his excitement knew no bounds. He was going to travel on a bus! He was the envy of the other children at first, but they were soon quietened as the elders told him all that he would have to do.

'We have chosen you because we have seen you are an obedient boy. Listen well. You are not ever to leave these old-ones you are escorting, except when they send you on their errands.' They so piled on his duties that he was almost sorry that he had offered. But then the very best news came and he was comforted. His mother would be in the bus party too. She would help the grannies, who, in turn would care for some of the babies and toddlers, to relieve their mothers on the journey.

The great day started before dawn. The loading of the donkeys, sorting out the livestock, and the rousing of the very old and the very young, was almost finished by the time dawn streaked the sky. The younger men would set out first, driving the cows, with the calves that were strong enough to keep up. Smaller calves would go with the sheep and goats, along with their lambs and kids. The boys would carry the smaller lambs and kids. But the tiniest of the newborn lambs would be given to women to carry tucked in their cloths, nestling in front if they had a baby on their back.

The procession set off slowly. Donkeys are stubborn and not easy to drive, so they needed to be whistled at and encouraged to keep going. Sheep, being herded along unfamiliar paths, kept straying. Lemayan enjoyed using his skill of throwing his knobbed stick so as to hit the ground just on the far side of the stray, nudging it gently back to the flock.

The old folk shuffled slowly along, but their journey would only take about three hours. Then they, with Lemayan and his mother would all rest for the next two days before they boarded the bus, while the others walked their weary way towards good pastures.

Going to a New World

'Run to that shop and buy me some tobacco to chew!' one old man ordered, handing Lemayan a shilling.

'Get some for me too and some 'emakat' (rock-soda) to chew with it,' another grandfather ordered.

Lemayan had never bought anything in a shop before, but having managed the first job, he enjoyed being sent for this and that. The mothers were busy finding places to sleep for themselves and the old ones, buying maize meal, tea and sugar to take to their hostesses. Lemayan, with his mother nearby, felt safe and secure and slept well.

The next day he found he had nothing to do. The old folk, having all they needed, just lay in the sun and dozed. Lemayan met some boys from a nearby village. He heard that they were on their way to school. So he wandered towards school with them, just for the company, but he soon lost interest.

A bell rang, the boys ran, they stood in straight lines, apparently afraid of the teacher who walked around, carrying a little stick, looking the boys up and down. Some were sent off to wash their feet. Some were scolded for wearing dirty shirts. Then the school children sang a song that Lemayan didn't know. The children all saluted as one of the big boys pulled a string and a flag was raised. Lemayan didn't understand what they were doing, but it didn't seem very interesting. When at last they filed into the school to sit there all day, Lemayan wandered off, glad that he had escaped being sent to that dreaded place called 'school.'

He preferred sitting at the side of the road, watching for any buses, cars or lorries that might come by. He wondered what it would be like, the next day, when he himself would travel on a bus!

The next morning it was difficult to gather everyone but when the bus eventually arrived, they were all ready – it was just as well, as the bus driver was impatient, annoyed about getting doddery grandfathers, and screaming children up into his bus. The children's screams became even louder when the bus started with a terrifying noise, and proceeded with frightening shaking rattling and bumping. But gradually as new sights flashed by them, the fear turned into interest. Later, looking forward to meeting up with friends and family - those who had done this long journey on foot – they became very excited.

But the mothers had many worries. 'Will someone be there to meet us?' 'How will we find where they have camped?' 'What if they haven't arrived yet?' 'Will they have made an enclosure for the cattle?' As they looked out on to the treeless plains, other worries were added. 'Where will we find bushes to use for fencing?' and, 'Where are sticks in this treeless land, to build new houses?' These and many other questions were tossed around as they neared the end of the journey. The buildings of the city, Nairobi, loomed tall and white on the horizon, but those were of no interest.

The bus stopped. The bus driver got up with a smile. 'This is where I was told to leave you all. Gather your loads and children and get out!' 'Come on, hurry up!' he added as they simply stared at him and then stared out of the windows. There was no one waiting for them and nothing to see! Reluctantly they gathered the children, roused the old folk and started descending. Eventually, when everything and everyone was off, the bus rattled away and a motley group of bewildered people stood about in a daze, not knowing where to go or what to do.

'Look! Over there!' Lemayan shouted in relief. His sharp eyes always alert, spotted two young men racing over the flat plain towards them. All eyes turned to look where he pointed.

'It's Kipeen and Leboo!' Lemayan exclaimed excitedly, recognising two of their warriors fast approaching. Worried looks changed to smiles of relief.

There was much shaking of hands, greetings, and 'eating the news'. The two young men first gave their good news. 'Yes, our journey was good. No difficulties. Everyone is fine. Yes, we arrived here last evening safely. No, no troubles.' Bad news is never blurted out at first meeting, so everyone was politely waiting to find out what the news really was. The young men started to look a bit uncomfortable as the exchange of questions and answers went on.

'Well, there are a few difficulties,' they admitted at last. 'So many herds have migrated to this area that the grazing is nearly finished. So many have

tried to make enclosures for their cattle that there
is not a bush left in miles. No one slept last night.
Lions in the nearby Nairobi Game Park have got
the news of easy prey.'

They all trailed wearily across the bare plain.
They had expected green grass, and space to
settle. Instead the whole area was littered with the
roughly made shelters and thorn fences of people,
like themselves, who had fled the drought. There
was little grazing left and absolutely no building
material at all.

The old folk were led to the little shelters of
skins the warriors had erected, and were given
'nturinki' to drink, tea, thick with sugar but no
milk. The small children were brought in and given
the little milk there was, and then old and young
settled dejectedly to sleep. Those in between old
and young sat about listlessly discussing what to
do, where to go.

No one slept that night. The mothers talked long
into the night about how to feed their families. The
warriors kept alert in the dark guarding the cattle,
sheep, goats and donkeys. With no enclosures, the
displaced animals could easily wander off. With no
enclosures, a lion's roar would scatter the cattle
into the dark in panic. A jackal's bark, or hyena's
eerie laugh would send the sheep and goats
panicking too.

The elders did what elders always do – talked
and talked, endlessly. There seemed no solution
to their problems. But by dawn a decision was
reached. They would move two hours further
away from Nairobi, where some of the stunted
whistling-thorn bushes still survived and where
the grass was not yet all gone.

Lemayan and the other children were eager for more adventures. But the men were anxious about the cattle and the women were worried about feeding their families. Some young men had gone ahead to sell a few thin sheep and goats. The mothers, disappointed at the little money that resulted, bought maize meal, potatoes, fat, onions, even some greens – all strange foods, eaten only in times of famine – plus of course tea and sugar!

Arriving at the new site, at first the children thought setting up camp was fun. They felt very important dragging the thorn branches the men cut, to where other men were skilfully making the fence to protect them all. But with many scratches on their arms and thorns in their little bare feet they soon lost interest. Food was the only thing that cheered everyone up – for a while.

Work over, the men drifted to the trading centre to find the beer-shop for refreshment. The warriors secretly took a little blood from some of the stronger steers to drink. The tired women, with small children all asleep, chatted over mugs of tea and felt refreshed.

Lemayan felt unsettled as he lay outside under the stars. Things were so different here. He longed for home. He also wondered about the clouds of little white butterflies he had seen everywhere in this strange new world. He wondered vaguely what they were.

Lemayan's World Saddened

The next morning Lemayan wandered about looking for something to do.

There was none of the accustomed milking to do in the early morning. Calves and lambs were all with their mothers and had already had their scanty breakfast. The men separated the adult stock from their young and took them away to graze. Lemayan wandered to and fro, feeling bored.

Then suddenly he saw such a strange thing - so strange that, in his surprise, he rushed up to a group of elders who were sitting talking gravely, and interrupted them, a thing a child should never do.

'Loo Papa!' (O Fathers!) he cried, 'Come and see! The ground is moving and the grass is disappearing!' Knowing that Lemayan was usually a respectful boy, they forgave him the interruption. They rose slowly, hitched up their blankets and sauntered over. Yes, the ground was moving, seething like water just before it boils, or like the shimmer on the horizon on a very hot day. The seething was moving forward! Then someone noticed that on the ground from which this strange sight had moved, there was not a tiniest, least spike of green left.

'Army worm!' Lemayan's father declared. 'I saw them once when I was a boy. They come in their millions and eat all the new grass, till not a blade is left. They hatched out from those white butterflies we have noticed. If the cattle eat them in any quantity they will die, especially in their present weak state.'

The men stared at each other in dismay. What could they do? Where would they go? They had come all this way, looking for grass. They had found less than they had hoped for and now that was fast disappearing under this new plague! What could they do?

They sent urgently for the cattle to be driven back into the enclosure before they ate too many of those fatal worms. The children came running out to see what was happening, found they were squashing multitudes of caterpillars under their bare feet and ran back in disgust.

That night the elders made the hardest decision of their lives. They would keep one young bull, two

heifers still in prime condition, a strong healthy ram and the three best young ewes. This breeding stock they would preserve for the future rebuilding of the herds. There was, not too far away, a holding ground where cattle could be cared for in emergencies. Water, medicines, fodder all had to be paid for, but their future would be safe. The rest of their cattle and sheep would be taken to the Kenya Meat Commission for sale before they got thinner or died.

Lemayan was heartbroken. Their beloved cattle killed for meat! Should we kill the ones we love? His heart was rebellious. It was Enkai's fault. Why hadn't he sent rain? Or was Enkai dead? Had the God who loved the Maasai died? Or did he just not care any longer?

Lemayan was not the only one heart-broken. His venerable old great grandfather, hearing of the tragedy, lay gazing into the fire till he fell asleep. In the morning they found that it was his last sleep. Without cattle life had no purpose and a Maasai had no identity. The whole group felt great sorrow, but it was not allowed expression. Anyone breaking down, or starting to wail was sternly told, 'Teena enkoshoke!' (literally, 'Tie up your stomach!' meaning, 'Control your emotions!') Giving way to wailing, it was felt, made the sorrow too great to bear.

Great honour and love was expressed towards this very old, respected man. New sandals cut from rawhide were put on his feet, to help him on his long, last journey. He was buried in a shallow grave under a shady tree and stones were piled over the grave. Any who pass by in days to come will toss more stones onto the pile and this will remain as a memorial to the honoured one.

So, to Lemayan's sorrow, the cattle and sheep were sold. The dejected company went on their weary way to the holding ground, where they left the breeding stock. Payment was made for six months care of those precious animals. The warriors set off home, ashamed to be driving only goats, no cattle at all! Only the very oldest and weakest of the company were put on the bus. Money must be stretched as far as possible. Food would have to be bought for many months to come. Lemayan and his mother were among those who walked those dreary miles back to an empty village

Lemayan's Question Answered

For Lemayan, life back in his home village had no flavour, like the uninteresting 'ugali' that was their food these days. It filled his stomach, but with no enjoyment. He lay around a lot, so unlike the active adventurous boy he had been. His body ached. He felt hot one minute and cold the next. He didn't want to eat the tasteless ugali' – he said it scratched his throat. But as zest had gone out of life for everyone, no one particularly noticed Lemayan's troubles.

One day, in his misery, he blurted out to his father, 'Papa, that Enkai you tell us about, whom you said loved us Maasai and gave us our cattle, has he stopped loving us? Why has he withheld the rain? Why has he let our cattle starve? Or has he died?'

Father looked at his son with compassion. His boy, who had a special love for the glory of the Maasai, their cattle! His son, who had pledged his love and life to the care of Enkai's gift, must be feeling very deeply the losses they had suffered. Also he had loved the old one dearly. But blaming and doubting the Great Enkai did not seem right. Then he remembered a story that would help his troubled boy.

'Son, Enkai is good. He gives us life and, in his time, he takes life. He sends rain and we thank him; he withholds rain and we don't understand. This evening I will tell you a story - a story of long ago. Call the other children later and I will tell it to all of you. It will help everyone to understand why people die.

'Etii apa,' Father started. The children had all gathered, bright-eyed and eager for a story, yet solemnly sensing that this was a serious tale. They were ready for the grunt that was expected at every pause in the storyteller's voice.

'Once upon a time there was a man called Leeyio. Enkai loved him and wanted him to live forever. One day Enkai came to him and said, 'That which I say to you today is very important. Listen carefully and do exactly as I say. The very next time someone dies, go outside into the night; gaze up at the moon and say:

'Moon die and stay away,

Man die and come back to life.'

'One day a child died and Leeyio remembered the Great One's words. He went out into the night and gazed up at the moon. It was round and silver and very beautiful. Its shining light transformed every object into a thing of beauty. He thought of life without a moon. No light to show the way to the traveller! No light to shine on celebrations of joy that go on far into the night! No protection at night from thieves, human and animal! He could not bring himself to say the words Enkai had given him. He thought, 'The child who has died was of a poor man of no importance, he will have many others.' So he lifted up his voice and said the fatal words,

'Man die and stay away,

Moon die and come back to life.'

'And so it was. People died and never returned to life. The beautiful moon 'died' every four weeks, but returned, young and new, without fail.

Some time later Leeyio's son died, his favourite first-born son. In an agony of sorrow he went out into the night. He looked at the moon, bright and serenely silver and cried out, in desperation

'Moon die and stay away,
Man die and come back to life.'

'Enkai's voice came solemnly from heaven. 'It is too late! You did not obey me when I gave you my message. You yourself said, 'Moon die and come back to life' and so it will always be. The moon will die. After three days the donkeys will bray in joy, because they see it first. Then in the evening of the fourth day you too will see the little sickle of the moon reborn. It will always come back to life, but man will always stay away. Your words have come too late.'

'So children, do not blame Enkai. Death came because of man's disobedience. Enkai wanted to give man life and man disobeyed. God also sorrows when one of us dies.

It is finished,' he said, referring to his story, but it also completed his explanation of why we all will die one day.

Lemayan went to bed and to sleep that night, wiser but not comforted, with his body still aching. He wondered if it was his time to die. He would not greatly mind. There did not seem much left to live for.

Lemayan's Big Trouble

After the many sorrows and hardships, Lemayan's parents eventually woke up to the seriousness of their dear child's illness. The fever and sore throat had left him, but he remained weak and listless.

'You know how much he loved the cattle,' Father said as he and Mother discussed the sad change in their promising son. 'He is just pining for the animals he loved so much. The 'sleeping' of the aged one also lies heavy on his heart. Leave him, he'll get over it, and come to life again soon.'

But Mother was not so sure. Sorrow affected the heart, not the legs. His left leg ached day and night. A Maasai does not admit pain, but her mother-heart knew about it. When there was no one to see, he would allow her to stroke, stretch and massage his aching limb, which she did lovingly, for many hours. But the light had gone out in her beloved boy. He just wanted to lie in the sun, curled up and miserable.

'We'll have to take him to the 'oloiboni' (the prophet). Perhaps there is a curse or some evil involved,' Father stated one day. But such a visit required goats and money to take to that one. Goats and money were very scarce these days. Anyway he lived far away, too far away for a sick child to walk there.

One day they received a welcome message

that might relieve their burden about food. 'The two white women from the Girl's School at the mission, will be coming on the day called Jumamosi (Saturday) to the borehole with some maize-meal and powdered milk for needy families' – was the message that gave them hope.

Men are too proud to admit they need help. Food is women's concern. So the women were only too glad to walk any distance to get food, and so eke out their fast dwindling money.

Early on Saturday morning the mothers set off with their sisal woven baskets and cloth bags and an empty tin or two – they were not too sure what they would be given, nor how much.

After an hour's walk they arrived where the 'tinka' (a diesel water-pump) was. As there were few cattle to water these days, and very little money for fuel, the pump was silent and the whole place, usually

a busy centre of activity, was deserted. Gradually women trickled in from different directions. There were many greetings among friends and relatives, and even strangers greeted each other. They all felt a common bond – food for their hungry children.

After a while they heard the approach of a vehicle. There was a stir of excitement; what would they be given? They were a bit disappointed when just one Kombi arrived. Would that carry all that they had hoped for? The two white women and their helpers climbed out and set up their table and chairs. The helpers, two young smiling Maasai men, beckoned the crowd to draw near to listen.

One of the white women, who said her name was Ng'oto Ntoyie (Mother of Girls) started talking, greeting them and introducing themselves and the purpose of their visit. There was giggling and

nudging and looking at each other in surprise – the white woman was talking their language! Not quite like a real Maasai, but they could understand when they got over their surprise and listened.

'We have brought you some powdered milk for your children. A lorry is on its way bringing many sacks of maize-meal.' A mutter of excitement spread through the crowd as they heard of the lorry. There would be enough for everyone!

'This milk powder is not for babies,' Ng'oto Ntoyie continued. 'You must go on feeding the tiny ones from your own breasts. This milk is for adding to the porridge you cook for the children. And don't let the grannies take all the milk to put in their tea!' The last remark was greeted with a knowing laugh, as they all knew that that was exactly what would happen!

'Now, we will call you, a few at a time, to write down your name and the number of children you are feeding at home, on a card. You will take the card to those men over there,' Ng'oto Ntoyie explained. 'They will then give you milk powder, according to your need. Keep the card to use again, when the lorry with the maize meal comes.'

It seemed so easy and clear to Ng'oto Ntoyie and Kokoo Ilmurran (Grandmother of the Warriors, the other white woman) but oh, so difficult to the mothers. It is not the custom for a woman to say her own name. So, with embarrassed giggling they'd nudge another woman to tell this inquisitive white woman what her name was. No one knew how many children they had! Children were people, not numbers. So what seemed a simple question, 'How many children do you have at home with you?' led to lengthy explanations.

Ng'oto Ntoyie listened carefully to the first woman, and wrote '2' on the card. Of her six children, one was married, a warrior was not eligible for milk, a boy was away at boarding school, and her last-born was a small baby. So when it was decreed that she therefore had only two children due a ration of milk she was puzzled. Surely she had more than two children?

They eventually got through the cards and the milk distribution, and still the lorry had not arrived. The two white women hoped that this was a good chance, while the mothers were waiting, to tell them about Jesus. Probably most of them had never heard about Him.

One of the men first stood up and explained what they planned to do. Then said, 'Let us pray and thank God for the food he has sent for your children. Be quiet and close your eyes.'

This brought a buzz of puzzled talking. Close their eyes? Why? Some, a bit more knowledgeable, told the others, 'Just put your hands over your eyes, they'll think you are shutting your eyes, but you can peep between your fingers!' So the prayer was prayed and a loud 'eesai' (amen) was said, but not a hand moved.

'You can open your eyes now.' Some obeyed, and then they told the others that they were now allowed to stop pretending to have their eyes closed. They found the ways of these people strange but many decided that next time they would really close their eyes because nothing much had happened while they were just pretending. Lemayan's mother noticed that the man praying had ended with the words, 'In the name of Jesus, the Son of God.' She knew all about God, but she certainly had never heard that he had a son!

However, before there was time to tell them about Jesus, the Son of God, the lorry arrived and all else was forgotten. Before the maize meal was distributed, an announcement was made, and repeated till all had heard and understood.

'Next month some Nurses are coming on the day the food is distributed. You must bring all your small children, those who still have their baby teeth. The Nurses want to give your children the medicine that stops children getting polio - that sickness that makes their legs weak and useless. But don't frighten the children. It is not a 'sindano' - a needle!' Children all scream at the word sindano.

'Also, if you have any sick children, or very thin children, bring them too. They will examine them and treat them, without you having to pay.' The last words caused a buzz of talking and interest. The Flying Doctor Mobile Team would have a good attendance when they came next month. There would be milk, food and medicine, all together on one day, and even a prayer to someone called Jesus.

But Mother of Lemayan went home with a heavy heart. She realised now what was wrong with her precious boy, the one who loved to run and play and herd the calves. He had polio, that sickness that made legs die and become useless. He would never walk again, never run after the stray calves. The medicine had come too late for Lemayan.

A Ray of Hope

Lemayan decided that he hated Enkai. The Great One who gave them cattle to love and cherish and then killed them by holding back the rain. Enkai who made him strong and then struck him down with a sickness that caused his left leg to wither and die. He would never walk again. Never run again. Never go out proudly with his father's cattle in search of water and far-off grazing, when he got bigger. He would never be a warrior. He was unclean, blemished, crippled. 'Fit only for school,' he thought, with loathing.

They did not know, but he had heard his father and mother discussing the things that had been said at the tinka. They had forgotten about him, huddled on his alcove bed, in the dark. They had even said that it was sad that the medicine had come too late for Lemayan. There was nothing to do. It was hopeless. Too late!

But he was a Maasai. Maasai are never cowards. They rise up and defeat their enemies. So he determined he would try to walk. He would force his leg to work. So he tried, but however much he tried, the leg would not obey him! He couldn't even straighten it. It stayed bent at the knee, with his foot flopping down. He tried to force his joints with his hands but that was painful, and did nothing anyway. His father noticed him trying and failing, and his heart bled for his precious son.

Then he had an idea. He would make some crutches. He knew their shape.

So one day, with his sharp two-edged sword strapped to his side, Father went off into the bush. He searched the stunted thorn trees for a branch with a good wide-open fork, with another branch growing out at a child's arms-length below, at right angles to the fork. He cut another the same, and, at home, peeled and smoothed them carefully.

'Ero, (my boy) wake up, I have something for you!' Lemayan was lying in the sun, feeling miserable, but he sat up when his father called.

'Son,' Father said, 'we Maasai are brave people. We don't give up when troubles come. We are fighters. We defeat our enemies.' Father's voice was stern. Lemayan sat up straighter, and felt embarrassed because he could not stand respectfully before his father. But Father guessed his feeling and squatted down next to him.

'Son,' he said, 'you have been very ill and we have been very worried and sad and puzzled about your sickness. At first I thought you were just grieving. But when your mother told me of your fever and pain I knew it was more than sorrow. Now we know what has happened. This polio has attacked you and your leg has become weak. We must face it as a Maasai faces his enemy. What Maasai has ever turned his back on his enemy and run away? I have two 'spears' here for you that you can use in fighting this enemy that has attacked your leg.' And with those puzzling words Father produced the two crutches he had made.

Lemayan looked bewildered. Spears? 'Father, what are these things that you call spears for me? What enemy can I fight with those strange looking sticks?' For answer Father lifted Lemayan, holding him under his armpits, to a standing position, steadying him firmly.

'Lean back against the house so you won't fall,' said Father, 'I want to measure this 'spear' against you, from the ground to your 'kitikit' (armpit).' Father did this quickly, cut off the few extra inches of the stick so that the forked end exactly reached the armpit. Then he cut the other to be the same length.

'Lift you left arm, Son!' Father commanded and promptly eased the forked end under his arm. 'Hold this little branch with your left hand. Now let's put the other one under your other kitikit. Hold them both. Lean on them. Now you can stand by yourself! You will even be able to walk, when you learn how to use these new 'legs' of yours. I called them 'spears' because with them you will be able to defeat the weakness of your leg. You will walk again using these things. Their real name is 'indirman' (crutches).'

Despair left Lemayan! For the moment, it felt like a thick mist lifting and the sun shining on him. His father loved him and cared about him. He might even be able to hobble about with these crutches that his father had so lovingly fashioned for him. It was true what Father had said, 'What Maasai ever turned his back to the enemy!' He hoisted himself up with difficulty, put the crutches in position, tried again, and fell! Determined, he did this again and again. Then it happened! Planting the crutches in front, he leant hard on them and swung his legs forward. He did it again - sticks forward, legs forward, – till he swung his legs too far forwards and fell over backwards.

He saw his mother coming back home, carrying a load of firewood, and quickly crawled back to where he usually lay. When Mother brought him a mug of steaming porridge fortified with powdered milk, he hid his excitement and accepted it with his usual listless thanks. Perhaps Mother caught a new gleam in his eyes but she said nothing.

He decided he was not going to let anybody see him trying to walk with his new crutches until he could do it well, with no falls. He would give them a surprise! But perhaps the family caught on to what was happening because he noticed that in the next few days, they all seemed to find odd jobs to do in other places - busy with the goats, firewood, water, washing clothes at the river. He had lots of time to practise his walking. The rhythm was - crutch, crutch, right, left.........over and over for hours.

The day came when he was ready. He told his mother, who told his father, who called his brothers and sisters, that he had something to show them. They all gathered outside, pretending they didn't know what this was all about. Feeling very important, but a bit nervous, he set the stage.

Standing in the doorway of the house, he asked them politely, 'Will you all please go away and stand at the 'enkishomi (the open gateway in the thorn fence)?' His great moment had come. Shakily at first but then with more confidence, he walked slowly across the ground towards them. His brothers and sisters clapped joyously. Father and Mother stretched out their arms anxiously towards him. He didn't mind falling when he arrived because he fell right into Mother's happy embrace. He enjoyed the praise and excitement and joy of everyone but his father's words made him proud.

'Well done, my brave warrior!'

Hope mixed with Fear

So, when the wonderful day dawned to go to Tinka with all the children, to see that Flying Doctor Mobile Team, Lemayan did not need to be carried, he was able to walk there. He was slow but he kept up with flustered mothers carrying babies, dragging reluctant toddlers and catching over-excited children.

What a cavalcade that was! Every woman in the community, plus all their big daughters, were needed to help carry the maize-meal and milk powder they were expecting to be given. All the babies and small children were carried or pulled along – no one was to be left out of getting free medicine. Everyone now realised the importance of the medicine for preventing the sickness that had struck Lemayan. Nearly all the old folk also joined in the exodus – each could think up some ailment. It was not often that those far out in the villages had the chance of some comforting treatment for their many aches and pains.

Robbie and Rosemary, the two English nurses in the Flying Doctor Mobile Team, were soon very busy trying to coax frightened children to open their mouths for the little squirt of Anti-Polio Vaccine each was to receive. Lemayan joined the queue, hoping that that medicine might heal his leg. But his father spoke up for him, through the driver of the Land Rover, who was interpreting for these nurses who knew only a little of the language.

'My boy has had this disease you are trying to prevent. Are you able to do anything to help him?' he asked, pushing Lemayan forward. When the nurses saw Lemayan, they seemed very pleased and excited.

'Who made those excellent crutches?' they exclaimed. 'Has he walked here today using them?' Father was commended and Lemayan was very proud.

'Yes, I made the crutches as well as I could, but it was the boy who taught himself to walk.' Lemayan glowed to hear his father's pride in him. 'But,' continued father, 'can you do anything to straighten his leg?'

'Yes, there is a lot we can do for him!' The nurses seemed very glad at the prospect of helping him. Lemayan was puzzled. They didn't know him. They had never even seen him before!

'Wait until we have finished with this line of children and until those others have finished giving out milk powder. Please don't get tired of waiting. We have a lot to tell you. He can be helped.' Father and Lemayan wandered off. They didn't mind waiting, but they wondered, each one in his-own way, what kind of help these white ladies were thinking up.

While he was waiting, Lemayan drifted over to where he saw a group of people gathered under a tree. Perhaps there was something interesting happening. There was!

The people were all listening to a voice coming out of a bright-red flat box that had a black plate spinning on it. A man was turning a little handle on the side of the box. The voice was speaking Maasai, but how a person could be inside that little box was beyond Lemayan's understanding. Then the man stopped turning the handle and the voice stopped. The man took the plate off, put another one on, and started turning the handle again. This time Lemayan was really puzzled. The Maasai-talking voice was now accompanied by a whole flock of sheep bleating! But soon he forgot his surprise and was caught by what the man was saying.

He told a story of a man who had many sheep - those you could hear bleating in the box. He told that in the evening, he had discovered to his dismay, that one of his precious sheep was lost. Lemayan listened with great interest. Some lazy shepherds leave lost sheep out in the night and only go the next morning to look for them. He, Lemayan, would never do that! The poor sheep would be frightened. A hyena might hear it crying and come and kill and eat it. What would the man in the box say? He heard with relief that the box-man felt just the same. After quickly penning the rest of the sheep, he went off into the night to look for the lost one. He did not give up. He looked for it until he found it. Then He picked up the frightened sheep and carried it over his shoulders, and the whole village was happy when he came back with his sheep safe and sound. A good story, Lemayan thought.

But there was more. The voice said that Jesus, God's Son, was our shepherd, a good loving, caring shepherd, who was looking for us and wanted to carry us and put us in his flock to care for us every day. Lemayan remembered that wonderful time, when he, as a little boy, had taken a lamb in his arms and held it to his heart. He remembered how love for that lamb had welled up in his heart. Did this Jesus, whom they said was the son of the great Enkai, love him, as he had loved that lamb? Lemayan felt he needed some loving and carrying these days with this stupid useless leg of his.

As he was thinking about this, his brother came running to call him. 'They have been looking for you everywhere. Father and Mother have been talking with those white women. It sounds as if they are going to take you away somewhere and cut off your bad leg! You'd better get there quickly!'

Lemayan's first thought was to run away and hide. But then he remembered that he couldn't run. Also, Father had reminded him that Maasai were brave and didn't run away. He stomped to where the group sat deciding his future. He firmly laid down rules in his mind as he approached. 'I won't go anywhere but home, and I won't have my leg cut off!'

He was greeted with happy smiles and congratulations on how well he could walk. His Father beckoned him to come and share the box he was sitting on. He felt safe there. 'That white woman over there, she has something to tell you. Your mother and I have heard and are happy. Listen well.'

'Lemayan,' Ng'oto Ntoyie started, (She knows my name! She is trying to trap me, he thought) 'we are very sorry you had that sickness that has killed your leg.' (Ai! She's talking my language! I can understand what she is saying! His fear increased along with his surprise.) 'But we have a place, a very nice place, at Kajiado where there are other children like you who have been helped.' (And all had their legs cut off?) 'We have taken them to hospital and the doctor (has cut off their legs! Lemayan's fear completed her sentence silently) has straightened their legs. They have come back with 'simiti' or cement on the weak legs to keep them straight. When the simiti is taken off then they are fitted with boots, with irons to keep the weak legs straight. When they can walk well, they stay with us to go to school. There are many Maasai boys like you there, and soon you will be running and playing football with them,' Ng'oto Ntoyie finished, not realising that Lemayan hated the very thought of school, and didn't know what the game of football was anyway.

After much discussion it was decided that Father would go back with the white ladies to Kajiado to see this place, to talk with the Maasai people who worked there, to check whether the place was worthy of his very precious son. (I hope he finds out whether the other children all still have both their legs, added Lemayan silently again.)

'Let us pray now to our Great Father Enkai,' added Noto Ntoyie, 'He loves Lemayan, and wants to bless him.' And with that everyone, except the fearful, suspicious Lemayan, reverently closed their eyes as the white woman prayed – for God's blessing on Lemayan and wisdom for his father in decisions. Then she ended her prayer with the words, 'In the name of Jesus our Good Shepherd who loves us all, children especially.'

'There again, that Jesus, that Good Shepherd, who carries his lambs,' thought Lemayan. 'He would be glad to know more about him – but not at the expense of a leg!'

Into an Unknown World

Much as he loved his father, Lemayan dreaded his return. The thought of leaving home, leaving his family, leaving everything familiar, made his tummy turn over in fear. But fear was not allowed in a Maasai boy. Moreover, home was no longer the familiar place he knew. No cattle, just a few goats to tend. Many boys, stronger than he, could do that job. He was useless!

Perhaps, in the new place, he could just get his leg fixed quickly and come home again – but to what? The bait that Ng'oto Ntoyie had given of school and football had no allure to him. He hated the idea of school, and didn't know what the game of football was. He thought miserably that he was one of those useless boys who were sent away to school because they were no good for anything else.

So it was a sullen, dejected boy that Father found when, after a few days, he came home, full of joy at what he had seen at the 'Enkaji oo Nkera' (the House of Children).

'It is a good place,' he stated, 'full of Maasai children, well looked after by women of our people. The children are all well fed and happy, very agile on crutches, with irons strapped to their legs and strong boots on their feet.' Lemayan remembered his first fear.

'Do the children all have two legs? Have any had their useless leg cut off?' Lemayan asked anxiously. Father was puzzled by this strange question but answered reassuringly.

'No, my boy, no one has had any legs cut off. Several were taken to hospital but came back with both their legs straight and better than they were before.' Lemayan was a bit ashamed of the silly fear planted in his mind by his brother. But there had been talk of cutting, and one never knew what these unknown white people might be up to!

Father went on explaining to Lemayan's mother all he had seen and heard at 'Enkaji oo Nkera'. Mother asked many anxious questions about food, care, sleeping, playmates and treatment for weak legs – all the questions a good mother would ask if her precious child was to leave her for a far-away place. At last they both agreed that it was a place fit for their son, their special son, to be cared for and helped.

His parents feared a protest at the decision, but Lemayan accepted his fate calmly, with no enthusiasm, but at least with no rebellion. His mother's heart was heavy. This special son of hers had been such a happy, lively, active boy, living life to the full. Would that spark ever come back?

There was little preparation needed, so the very next day Father set off, leading a scraggy goat, with a dismal Lemayan trudging behind him. Some of his friends, shouting goodbyes, were quite envious. They would like to be going off to the big new world, but Lemayan would gladly have changed places with them. It was a long walk for a seven-year-old, struggling on homemade crutches, to the place to catch the bus. On arrival they went to sell the goat at the little butcher shop. Then they slaked their thirst – Father, with a huge mug of beer and Lemayan, with an unfamiliar drink fizzing in a bottle called Coca Cola. But the real treat was a good chunk of roast goat that father and son enjoyed together as equals. Children don't normally eat with their fathers.

But Father was in a hurry to take him to the biggest 'duka' (shop) in the little town. 'I want to buy all the clothes and everything else that a boy going to school needs,' he demanded imperiously of the Asian shop owner. Soon Lemayan was dressed in khaki-coloured shorts and shirt, both rather stiff and far too big. Shoes were a problem because of his withered ankle, so they gave up on them. The shopkeeper also insisted that he needed a wooden

box, with a padlock, to keep his possessions in. Lemayan wondered what he would put in it, as he had on the only clothes he possessed. But when soap, a packet of Omo, a T-shirt, a few peppermints, a pencil, biro and handkerchief were added to the purchases, there was a box to put them into!

Lemayan remembered anxiously what Father had said to the shopkeeper: '...for a boy going to school.' He stated firmly to himself, 'I am not, no, I am not going to school. I am going to get my leg straightened, fitted with the things that will help me walk well – then I am coming home.' But he kept these thoughts to himself. One does not argue with one's father.

Very soon a bus rattled into the market place. Father saw him safely seated and said goodbye. Lemayan quailed at the thought of travelling alone, of getting off the bus alone, and of facing his new life alone. But Maasai boys are brave and he was seven years old – no longer a little boy. Father gave him a small skin bag with some shillings in it for his bus fare. The bus started with a roar and lurched forward and Father soon disappeared from view. The last link with home was gone. He had new strange clothes to wear, a new home to fit into, new friends to make and a new life to live – just for a while. He didn't know whether to be happy or sad, excited or afraid. Lemayan wondered what lay ahead of him at the place called Enkaji oo Nkera – officially called The Child Care Centre.

Mixed Feelings

After what seemed a very long way, the bus stopped and the bus-driver told him that this was where he was to get out. One of the passengers took his wooden box, put it on the ground and helped Lemayan down. He came reluctantly, wondering where to go and what to do. The bus left him with a roar and he wished he could run after it.

Suddenly he heard shouting and a gang of noisy boys came running, hopping, swinging on crutches, across the field to meet him. They gathered round him, noticing his very new clothes and homemade crutches with approval. A boy who used only one crutch took charge of his box. He hadn't expected any such welcome!

'A man who was here the other day, told us he would soon put his son on the bus to come to come to join us here,' one of the excited boys explained.

Another butted in, 'So while we have been playing football we have been watching out for the bus.'

'Where are you from?'
'What's your name?'
'How long ago did you get polio?'
'Have you been to school before?'

The questions came thick and fast. Everyone was trying to be friendly. Lemayan attempted to answer all their questions but they weren't really listening as they ushered him across the field towards some big buildings. A smiling woman, wearing Maasai-style dress, just like his mother always wore, came out, shooed the chattering boys back to their play and took Lemayan inside. He bowed his head before her to be greeted in the way all children greet an adult.

'Ng'asak Yeiyio,' (Greet me, Mother) he muttered politely. She gently placed her hand on his head and said, 'Layioni lai,' (My boy) He answered with 'Oe!' (Yes!) Then she greeted him with 'Supai!' (Greetings) and he received her greetings with the response, 'Epa!'

She led him to a table where they sat down on a long bench. Then she asked all the right questions – Of what clan was he? Of whose village was he? What was his father's family name? Which mother bore him? By the answers, she could identify his place in the structure of the tribe, his identity and importance. Just to say at first, 'I am Lemayan,' meant nothing. That he was Lemayan of so-and-so, born of the senior wife, of such-and-such a village of a specified clan, made him a valued, proud member of his community.

'Oh, my boy!' she acknowledged happily, 'Your mother is the daughter of my uncle's second wife.'

This made Lemayan feel at home. Here they lived in very different houses, had no cattle, no milking, no preparing of the gourds, but this woman was a true Maasai mother.

Just then a tall white woman came in. Her Maasai name, he later discovered, was Naado, the Tall One.

'Oh, here's our new boy,' she smiled at him kindly. 'What's his name?' They told her. 'Come here, Lemayan.' He hopped across the room on his crutches. She was so impressed with his homemade crutches and his mobility on them that she forgot all about greetings, as so often happens with white people. Instead, she put her arm around him and snuggled him to her, to make him feel welcome. He was glad other boys were not around. He was no longer a baby!

'Give him some tea to drink. He must be tired after his journey,' Naado instructed. 'When he has finished bring him to my office. I want to examine his leg because we have a trip into Nairobi tomorrow. We can get his treatment started soon. He is a big, bright boy – he should be in school as soon as possible.'

Lemayan liked being called 'big boy' and 'bright', and even the sound of going with her to the city he had seen in the distance last year. He wondered what the 'treatment' was. But the last statement, he knew he did not like. 'Let's just get my leg better and I'll go home,' he said to himself. School was not, no, not on his agenda!

The tea was sweet and very welcome, but it didn't taste like the tea his mother made. It lacked the nice smoky flavour that gourd-milk gives. While he was drinking it, another white woman came in. She was shorter and older and called Kokoo Lmurran (Granny of the Warriors). He recognised her from that first time at Tinka. She had been writing their cards for receiving the milk powder and maize meal.

'Where is Nemayan?' she asked. 'The boys playing football ran to tell me that a new child called Nemayan has arrived. I have been looking out some clothes for her.' She was holding a whole armful of pretty girl-clothes, from the parcels people in churches overseas had sent, to be given to children coming into the Child Care Centre.

The two women laughed and Lemayan felt embarrassed. His name with the 'n' sound in front was a girl's name! 'There is no Nemayan, Kokoo,' they explained, 'He is a boy. That smart young boy over there! He is Lemayan, one of your little warriors.' They all laughed together and Lemayan relaxed.

'Stand up, my Warrior! Let me see how tall you are, so that I can go and get boy- clothes for you from the cupboard,' Kokoo said. But when he stood up and she noticed his crutches, she was very excited.

'Oh! You are the boy we saw the other day at Tinka. I am so glad you have come. We have been praying you would join us here. God has answered our prayers.' Lemayan felt better now. He had been forgiven for not being a girl and Kokoo hurried off to find suitable clothes for him. He wondered why she had prayed for him, and why he needed more clothes than those that his father had bought him this morning. All that seemed a very long time ago.

After tea he was taken to Naado's office. She asked him many questions and wrote things in a book. She examined his leg. She got him to try moving it in different ways so that she could find out what parts were weak. She was still busy with this when Kokoo came back with unfamiliar clothes – two other garments to be worn inside his clothes. Also a shirt and pair of longs, of a soft material, called pyjamas. He was especially proud of the bright shirt and long trousers she gave him that he was to wear the next day to Nairobi. His mind was reeling from all that was going on.

Suddenly there was a loud noise. Naado hurried to the door and called a big boy to her. 'Kemendere, that is the supper bell ringing. Take this new boy, Lemayan, to supper and look after him. Then bring him back here. I'll give you sheets, a blanket and his clothes when you come back.'

This bigger boy, with both legs in irons and using two crutches, gave Lemayan a friendly smile and they set off to where that big bell was still ringing.

Lemayan felt shy of all the boys and girls rushing into the room. Everyone knew where to go and what to do. He was glad of Kemendere to guide him. The boys who had met him off the bus, smiled at him too, wanting to be friendly. Then a generous plateful of ugali was put before him as well as a bowlful of delicious stew. He piled into it with gusto and decided that this place was not too bad.

When the eating was over the Mamas cleared away the plates. Then everyone started singing and clapping. The songs were new to Lemayan, as was everything he was seeing and doing. But as he listened he heard that they were singing about Enkai and praising Him, and about God's Son, Yesu. Lemayan was soon clapping with everybody and even singing along too. As there was lots of repetition in the songs he caught on quickly.

The singing died down as one of the Mamas came in and started to talk to them. She asked the children if any of them remembered the words she had taught them the day before. Suddenly many of them put up one arm, waved it eagerly and shouted, 'Nanu, Nanu!' (Me, Me). He wondered why they waved their arms like that – it must be one of the silly things children learnt to do at that dreaded place called school.

The Mama then pointed to one girl who was waving her arm furiously. The girl stood up and said shyly, 'Jesus said, I am the Good Shepherd, the Good Shepherd gave his life for the sheep.' 'Good!' said the Mama, and they all repeated what she had said a few times, till Lemayan was also saying those words. Then the Mama told them the same story he had heard from that box with the plates that spoke his language – the story of the man who went after the lost sheep until he found it. Then she opened a little black thing that he learnt later was called a book, a special one that had God's words in it, called Osotua Nge'juk (New Testament). She asked Kemendere to read from the book and he read that same story again, about the man who went after his lost sheep until he found it.

'We are happy today,' Mama said, 'to welcome Lemayan to the Enkaji oo Nkera. Our Good Shepherd has sent him here, to bless him and help him to walk again.'

Everyone looked at him. Lemayan felt uncomfortable and was happier when she said, 'Let us pray,' because they closed their eyes then, except a few girls near him who were giggling the way girls do.

After he and Kemendere had collected the promised things from Naado's office, they went to the big room where the boys slept. Here Kemendere arranged the sheets and blanket on a bed which he was told he was to sleep on – alone! He had never covered himself with a sheet and blanket before. He had never slept by himself before. But what was most surprising was that he was told that those special clothes called pyjamas were to be worn in bed and only put on after he had washed! Why wear such smart clothes in bed, under a blanket? No one could see them!

Then came a playtime that Lemayan could enjoy. All the boys took off their boots and the irons from their legs and laid aside their crutches. They could no longer walk, but all had a great time crawling, chasing each other and playing on the floor that was covered with smooth, coloured squares. It was fun. He had wanted to play with his friends at home but he no longer could. He had longed to have his two strong legs again. In this place they were all the same. No one had strong legs here.

Soon Kemendere came to haul him off to wash. They went into a very small room where he took off his clothes and sat on a little chair. Kemendere scrubbed him all over with a rough, soapy cloth. Then he turned a little handle on the wall and water, lots of warm water, rained down on him from the roof. Lemayan enjoyed it. He turned to look up at where the water came from and the 'rain' washed all the soap off his face.

When he eventually crawled out he found all the other boys crawling in and out of the little washing rooms – all with nothing on. They went on playing, and drying themselves on other big cloths until Kemendere called out, 'Bedtime' and they all crawled to their beds, struggled into their pyjamas and, quite soon, climbed on to their beds, pulled the sheet and blankets up over their heads and went to sleep.

It took Lemayan longer. He fumbled with the sheet, pulled it up over his head and he lay down, thinking of all the strange and wonderful things that he had seen and done since this morning when he had left home. He missed the dark smoky hut. He missed a good long drink of sour milk from his very own gourd. But he wasn't hungry and he wasn't cold. Everyone had been very kind to him. He was happy and sad at the same time. He didn't want to be here, and yet he had enjoyed everything.

At last, he turned over to go to sleep, reciting the words he had learnt, 'Jesus said,' I am the Good Shepherd, the Good............' but he was asleep before he could finish the words.

A World Undreamed of!

'Wake up, Lemayan!' The Mama, who had talked about the Good Shepherd, was shaking him awake. 'Naado wants you to be ready to go with her to Nairobi in half an hour.' She found the clothes Kokoo had given him yesterday.

'Put these clothes on quickly and then come to the room where I gave you tea when you arrived.' He wondered why he couldn't go to Nairobi in what he was wearing, the things called pyjamas, but he obediently put on the other new clothes. Truly, now he was smart enough for the big city – except for the thing in the front of his trousers with lots of little teeth. He didn't know how to close that! But the mama dealt with it. She also wiped his face with a wet cloth, and smoothed down his crinkly hair with a brush – being clean seemed to be very important at this new place. Then she gave him a big mug of steaming porridge, sweet and milky – and, when he had finished drinking it, wiped his face again!

Another Mama came bustling in with two little girls and they were given porridge also. Then Naado came and took the three of them out to a big Land Rover. The other Mama got in the back to look after the girls and Lemayan was allowed to sit in front with Naado. He felt very important as they drove off. He feasted his eyes on all he saw – cattle and sheep grazing near the road, wild animals scattering at the sound of the car – familiar home sights.

Until they turned on to another road! Then his eyes opened wider as lorries, buses, cars of all shapes and sizes roared by them. But when they got into the part where the buildings were as high as mountains, he wanted to shut his eyes tight closed. The vehicles were so noisy and the houses so high he was sure he was in danger. He looked sideways at Naado and she looked quite calm and happy. The two little girls were crying loudly, but then, they were girls!

They arrived at the place called 'Sipitali' (Hospital) and got out of the Land Rover. Lemayan felt terrified of entering this huge unknown building. At least he wasn't fussing and sobbing like the girls were. He felt anxious when Naado left them sitting on a long bench with the Mama, but

she came back and took them to sit on another bench. Then she took him and the girls, one by one, to see the doctor.

The rest of the day passed in a haze, going here and there. Naado gave them bananas and mandasis to eat and an orange-looking drink called Fanta. The old fear was with him constantly. Were these people going to cut his leg off? There were children crying wherever they went but nowhere did he see a child who had had a leg cut off!

Later Naado took all of them aside where they could listen carefully. 'You three are going to sleep here in the hospital tonight.' At this the girls increased their sobs and Lemayan swallowed hard. 'Later, when you are in bed a nurse will give you tea and bread. Sleep well; there is nothing to be afraid of. You will not be given anything to eat or drink in the morning. The doctor is going to put you to sleep with his medicine. They will straighten your legs while you are sleeping. When you wake up you will find your weak legs will have hard white stone made of 'olturoto' all round your legs, keeping them straight. Mama and I will be with you when you wake up. Be brave.'

But it was hard for these three desolate children to be brave. Strange people dragged them off to be washed and put to bed. They couldn't understand what the nurses were saying to them. No one spoke their language. Everyone got impatient with them and treated them as if they were stupid. Only the people who went to school, or mixed with other tribes, spoke Kiswahili. But the three of them might well have been deaf for all they understood of what they were being told.

The girls sobbed themselves to sleep but Lemayan stared open-eyed into the dark for a long time, afraid of the next morning. Presently a man came to Lemayan's bed, picked him up and put him on another bed with wheels. This unknown man chatted to him as he wheeled him a long way to another room. Lemayan looked up into the man's face. He seemed kind, and smiled down at the silent boy trying to be brave. Surely nothing terrible would happen to him while there were nice friendly people about?

In this new room people looked strange because their mouths and noses were hidden behind little square green cloths, and with green caps on their heads, the only thing that showed were their eyes. One of these green men came, mumbled something and then pricked his arm with a needle. Soon he felt drowsy and tried very hard not to go to sleep – but he remembered nothing after that…

Dimly he heard Naado's voice. 'He's waking up.' True, he was struggling though a sort of mist. He felt funny. But it was reassuring, when he opened his eyes, to see Naado. The mama also spoke comforting words to him in his own language and he felt safe at last. Then he felt pain. Had they cut his leg off while he was sleeping! He reached down. No, his leg was still there! But as his hand went further towards his knee he found that his leg was wrapped up in stone. Naado saw him feeling his leg and spoke comfortingly to him.

'The doctor has made a little cut in the back of your knee so that he could straighten your leg. He put this 'simiti' (cement, the easiest explanation) to keep it straight. The simiti will also keep your foot in the right place for walking. After six weeks we'll cut it off.' Lemayian's eyes widened with fear. So they were, as he had feared all along, planning to cut off his leg!

'No, not your leg, silly boy!' Naado laughed gently, seeing the fear in his eyes, 'Only the simiti will come off. Then your leg will stay straight as you'll wear those irons and boots you saw the other boys have.' Thinking that he needed something nice to look forward to she added, 'Then you'll be able to go to school. And soon you'll be playing football with the other boys.'

So, they were doing all this to trap him! To put him in school! To kick a silly ball around! No! However kind they were, however nice the food was, he was not going to school. As soon as the plaster was off his leg and he had those irons and boots on, he was going home. Back to his village, back to the life he loved.

When he returned to the Child Care Centre, he treated every one with suspicion. They were all kind and friendly – yes, just to catch him for their silly school. The food was delicious and plentiful – yes, just to fatten him up like we fatten the sheep we plan to slaughter. He changed into a sullen, suspicious little boy. The worse he became, the friendlier and kinder everyone was to him. They thought he was just homesick, so they all tried their very best to be nice to him.

The worst day was when they tried to make him go to Nursery School with the little four and five-year-olds. 'The real school is too far for you to go with your leg in plaster. Go and learn with the little ones. Learn the numbers and the letters first, so you will be ready to go to big school next term,' Naado tried to reason with him. He said his leg was sore. The next day he had a headache. Every day he had some other excuse. So at last they left him to mope while the others were at school. Then, of course he felt lonely, bored and unhappy.

Then one wonderful day his father came to visit him.

Longing for Home

Lemayan, however, was not the happy boy Father expected to find. He was glad to see his father but otherwise was sullen and full of grumbles.

'Father, please take me home. I hate this place,' Lemayan pleaded.

'What's wrong with it?' Father asked. 'Are these people not good to you? Is the food not enough? Have you made no friends among the boys here?' Father tried to think of all the things that could have made his dear son so unhappy.

'No, Father,' he admitted, 'everyone is very kind. But they are only being kind because they are trying to trap me into going to school. The food is very good and more than I have ever eaten at home – but we never even get a taste of our lovely smoked sour milk. The boys want to be friends, but all they talk about is school, and they spend all their time, when they are not in school, kicking a silly big ball around the field.'

Father started to see light. He remembered how Lemayan had always dreaded the thought of school. The flocks and herds were his life.

'But do you go to school?' he queried.

'They tried to make me go to baby school,' Lemayan explained with disgust. 'The proper school for boys of my size is too far for me to go with this plaster on my leg. The baby school is not for me! The children there are just four or five years old. They already know their letters and can write their numbers. I don't want to go to school, but anyway I can't go to school with little children who know more than I do! Father, do you remember, long ago you promised that you would never make me go away to school? You said I would always stay with the cattle.'

Yes, Father remembered. He remembered his lively, active free boy who poured the love of his heart into the calves and lambs when he was tiny. He remembered his own pride as his son developed into the best herder in the village. But things were different now.

'But, my son, you are crippled now. With your weak leg, you would not be able to look after the herds. Remember too, we sold most of our

livestock. I am on my way now to see how our bull, those two heifers and the sheep are. We have had rain at home. If they are strong and healthy, I will drive them back to our village. But there are plenty of young men to care for them. If you came home you would have nothing to do.' Father talked long to his dear boy to make him understand the changed circumstances. But Lemayan was not to be moved.

'Father,' he stated firmly, 'if I am now useless, let me be useless at home.'

Father went off to see the mamas and had a long chat. Then they took him to Naado and they talked some more. Later he came back to his unhappy boy.

'Son,' Father brought his decision to Lemayan, 'we have decided that you stay here till the plaster

is taken off your leg. Then you will be fitted with the irons, boots and elbow-crutches. By the time you can walk really well with those things, it will be school holidays when all the children here go to their villages for four weeks. If you still do not want to go to school after those four weeks, you may stay at home. I won't break my promise to you, but I hope you'll change your mind.' He did not add that the Mamas and Naado had all said they were praying that God would change Lemayan's heart.

So Father left, and Lemayan felt satisfied. In a few weeks he would be home, drinking sour milk, in their dear smoky dark house with all the familiar sights and smells of home. He would be safe from the threat of school.

His Good Shepherd

'On Saturday after supper Ng'oto Ntoyie and Kokoo are coming to show us all a "senema".'

Mama announced this one evening after she had taken prayers in the dining room. 'Senema' derives from 'cinema', a grand name for the little filmstrips the missionaries often showed to make Bible stories more vivid.

There was great excitement. Not having even heard of television and never having seen a film, the filmstrips were a novelty. So on Saturday evening they had supper early. The Mamas cleaned the tables and swept up all the crumbs of 'ugali' accidentally dropped on the floor, and also all the bits of cabbage dropped deliberately by those children who still felt that eating leaves was for goats only.

Presently the two white Grannies bustled in with their equipment. 'Let the children sing some choruses while we get ready,' one of them suggested to the Mama who usually led prayers. Soon the room was ringing with loud singing from the eager youngsters. Even Lemayan sang heartily. He had learnt the songs quickly and loved this part of being in the House of Children. He thought wistfully that he might hear some more of the Good Shepherd that he loved hearing about. He too had been a good shepherd of his father's sheep.

At last all was ready. Kokoo sat next to the little machine. Ng'oto Ntoyie stood in front, beside a big white sheet that was hung up on the wall. She had a long thin stick in her hand. Was this to beat them if they were not quiet? The Maasai count it as an insult to be beaten by someone's hand. Maasai mothers always pick up a little stick and waggle it at a naughty child. But the stick Ng'oto Ntoyie was holding was for pointing at details of the pictures. She knew that it is rude, in Maasai culture, to point with a finger.

Kokoo turned the machine on. The lights were put off. All was dark except the bright light shining on the white sheet. The first picture was of a lot of animals, and a buzz broke out as the children tried to identify them - a rhino, a giraffe, a snake, a monkey, a hyena, an elephant and others. There was a long high wall, built of blocks like those of which the Child Care Centre was made. Ng'oto Ntoyie then explained that this was a story of those animals, who wanted very much to cross that wall, and were trying different ways to do it. The next pictures were of the rhino. It was not quite like the rhinos that they had seen, but, when one big boy said that perhaps it was a rhino from the neighbouring country of Tanzania, they were satisfied. The rhino was trying unsuccessfully to knock the wall down with his big sharp horn.

Then came the elephant also trying, in vain, to push the wall over. Next a monkey climbed up the giraffe's neck to gain height and attempted to climb to the top of that wall. The children laughed heartlessly at the picture of the monkey falling, somersaulting down to the ground. The snake tried burrowing under the wall, and they all laughed again at the snake's surprise when he came up, still on the same side of the wall where he had started. The hyena set off to find the end of the wall, but all in vain. He came back with his tongue hanging out and his tail between his legs, defeated.

'That wall is a picture of our sin, our disobedience to God,' Ng'oto Ntoyie explained. 'We are not able to get to God because of that wall called SIN that separates us. The animals tried to get to the other side. They all had their own skills and strengths, but failed. There is no way that we can cross that wall by ourselves. But, here is Good News! God has made a way for us.' The next picture showed that wall called SIN, but this time, with a little door in the shape of a cross.

'The cross of Jesus is the way God has made for us to get past that wall of sin, be forgiven and become God's own true children,' Ng'oto Ntoyie concluded.

The children then sang a quiet chorus while Kokoo did things with her little machine. Lemayan didn't sing. He was thinking, wondering what the 'cross of Jesus' was, and how it could make him a child of the Great Enkai.

'These next pictures are not fun ones,' Ng'oto Ntoyie warned. 'We laughed at those silly animals relying, in vain, on their own ability. These pictures you will see now are of true things that happened to Jesus, God's Son, when He was on earth. They show Jesus suffering - the things He suffered to get you and me through that wall of sin, and into His family.'

'Things He suffered for me!' Lemayan was surprised to hear that God's Son knew him! So he was all ears and eyes as the next filmstrip unwound.

There were many pictures - Jesus riding on a donkey, Jesus praying in the dark and angry people pointing fingers at Him. Then there was a horrible picture of Jesus being nailed to a piece of wood. Lemayan closed his eyes. He didn't like to look. He missed a few that followed, but when Ng'oto Ntoyie said, 'Jesus did this for you because He loved you!' he opened his eyes. There he saw Jesus on the cross. Blood had come from his hands and feet and side and Ng'oto Ntoyie said that He had died.

'Jesus did this because He loved you!' The words echoed in his heart. He felt tears come to his eyes. 'For Me?' he thought. 'All that pain, for me?' But he quickly wiped his eyes in case the other boys saw his tears.

The last filmstrip was about that very first story that he had heard at Tinka on that little black plate – the story of the Good Shepherd. He enjoyed that one. He identified with the shepherd's concern about one lost sheep. He was glad that he did not give up and understood his joy at finding it. He too would have carried it gladly over his shoulders, with love and rejoicing. Then he remembered the words from the Bible he had learnt on his first day at this place.

Jesus said, 'I am the Good Shepherd, the Good Shepherd gave His life for His sheep.'

The show was over. The lights were turned on and Kokoo started packing up her little machine. But Ng'oto Ntoyie still had something to say.

'Before we close with prayer, I want to tell you of something that happened long, long ago when I was young, about the age of…(she looked around at the children) … of Lemayan over there. I also had gone one evening to a place where we children were shown pictures of Jesus. I saw a picture of Jesus on the cross, and when the teacher said that He had suffered for me because He loved me, I cried. That night in my bed I prayed to Jesus. I thanked Him for loving me and dying for me. I asked Him to forgive my sins and make me His true child. Jesus heard my prayer, accepted me, and my Good Shepherd has cared for me ever since. You can do the same,' she added, 'you too can accept His love and become His child.'

She prayed and the children went back to their dormitories to get ready for bed. In all the fun and games of showering, playing and crawling about on the smooth floor, Lemayan did not forget the words he had heard. Soon he was in his pyjamas, safely in bed, with the sheet and blanket tightly over his head.

'Dear Jesus,' he murmured, 'thank you for loving me even when I hadn't ever heard of you. Thank you for dying for my sins. Please forgive me, make me your child and help me to follow you, my Good Shepherd, for ever.'

He went to sleep happy, dreaming that he was a lamb, at peace and loved, being cuddled in the arms of the Good Shepherd.

His Friend, Kemendere

'What has happened to you?' Kemendere asked Lemayan one afternoon, a few days after the senema. He had taken this new boy to his heart, and was glad to see that he seemed happier.

Kemendere was the prefect of the boys' dormitory. He was older than the other boys and had already had several years at school before he came to the Child Care Centre. He had had polio a few years back, had been put in hospital and left there. As he recovered, he had been fitted with braces on his legs and two clumsy iron crutches and discharged from hospital. His family were only too glad to let him go to a school in the town, as they saw no future for a badly crippled boy in the harsh life of cattle nomads. They found a distant relative in the town with whom he could stay, bought him school clothes and books, and wiped their hands of him.

After some time that relative moved and he had to look after himself. His boots wore out, he had outgrown his crutches and some of the straps on his braces were torn so that they scarcely supported his withered legs.

Then one wonderful day he had heard of the Child Care Centre and hope welled up in his heart. He prayed to Enkai then, as he had often prayed before when his family threw him out, and God had helped him.

'Naai! (O God!) Hear my cry to you! Let me get to that place of help. Hear me!' And Enkai heard.

The town in which Kemendere lived, Magadi, existed only because of the strange lake, down on the floor of the Great Rift Valley – Lake Magadi. The hot sun drying up the water leaves a crust of soda. Flamingos often are trapped, just by standing still too long in the water. A crust forms round their legs and leaves them helpless, unable to fly.

In some parts, that crust is so thick that huge machinery has been erected on it, which digs the rock-soda and puts it on lorries – yes, huge trucks can drive across the crust and take their loads to the specially designed railway trucks, which take the soda to a factory in the city.

Kemendere knew about that train. He knew it passed the town where the Child Care Centre was. So one day, during school holidays, he hobbled to the railroad terminus. He had no money for a ticket, but his obvious need softened the heart of the guard and he was allowed to sit on a box in the guard's van.

Arriving in the town, he struggled up the hill to the place of help that had been pointed out to him. He wondered what he would find. Would the people there receive him? Would they help him? He had no money, nothing.

He need not have feared. This was the answer that Enkai had prepared for him when he cried out in his need. A mama, working in the kitchen, seeing a crippled boy struggling up the path, hurried out to meet him – leaving the porridge bubbling on its own.

There was great excitement. Kemendere was the first child who had come on his own to look for help. His walking equipment was obviously too small, his boots broken out at the toes, with holes in the soles. He was received with joy and, in the next few days, Naado fitted him with boots and braces and with extendable aluminium elbow-crutches. Being the month of school holidays, most of the children had gone home, so the Mamas had lots of time to show love to this brave boy. They fed him generously. They also told him more about Enkai, who had answered his prayers, and about the Son of the Great God, Jesus, who had died for us all.

The welcome and the loving help given softened Kemendere's heart to the message about Jesus and soon he found new life. He felt happy and loved - loved not only by these kind people, but loved by Enkai Himself. He was determined to stay in this wonderful place forever.

One day, as the school holidays were coming to an end, Naado had come to talk to Kemendere.

'You attend the school in Magadi,' Naado started to explain. 'We hear you are already in Class 6. Here are some shillings for the train-fare to take you back home. Your parents must be worried and have been wondering where you are. You must go tomorrow. We are glad you came. When you grow out of your braces, or your boots wear out, come back in the school holidays and we'll help you. Back in Magadi, find a church where you will hear more about Jesus...' she went on talking but Kemendere was not listening. At last he got a chance to interrupt her.

'But I am staying here!' he insisted politely. 'I'm staying and will go to school here. I am not going back to Magadi.'

Naado was surprised. 'But you must go back! Your family don't know where you are.' She called Mama to come and reason with him. Then his story came out. His family didn't care where he was. They had thrown him out as useless. Recently he had been sleeping anywhere that a kind shopkeeper would give him a meal and space to sleep on the floor.

So Kemendere had stayed. They first sent him back on the train, with a return ticket. He got a transfer letter from his Headmaster, picked up a little bundle that contained his tattered school uniform and a few books and was back the next day. He hoped that the message he tried to send to his father, through someone who lived fairly near his old home, would, sometime, let his family know where he was. He hoped they still cared.

Kemendere had become a great help in the Child Care Centre. Having himself suffered, he was kind to new boys feeling homesick. Having been hungry, he influenced the others to appreciate the food, so different from their home diet. By his good example he influenced the behaviour of the younger boys. Now Lemayan had become his special concern. This new boy had been surly and uncooperative. But lately he seemed to have changed.

Kemendere repeated his question. 'Lemayan, you seem happier these last few days. What has happened to you?' He suspected what the answer was but wanted Lemayan to say it himself.

Lemayan was shy. 'Oh, it's just because I am soon going home,' he hedged. But Kemendere was not to be put off.

'No, that is not all,' he probed. 'You seem happy and at peace. You seem content to be here, and you are friendlier to everyone. Tell me, what has happened to you?'

Lemayan smiled. 'I am glad that you can see that I have changed,' he confessed. 'That night of the senema I asked Jesus, the Good Shepherd, to forgive me and come into my heart. I have become His child. That is why I am happy.'

At that moment Lemayan and Kemendere became brothers. The bigger boy taught his smaller new 'brother' more about Jesus, their Good Shepherd. Day by day Lemayan learnt more about how to follow Jesus. He listened closely to what was said at evening prayers. He learnt the songs well. He wanted to be able to teach the children in their home village the songs, even though he didn't yet know enough about Jesus to explain his new faith.

'I wish you could come home with me, Kemendere,' Lemayan said. Thinking about going home, he wondered what his father's reaction would be to these new words about Jesus. Then, talking with Kemendere, he discovered that his friend had nowhere to go for his school holidays, so Lemayan invited him to his home for the four weeks. Together, things would be much easier. Kemendere would be able to explain about Jesus to the people at home. He could also read the little black book to them, the book that had God's message in it.

By the time school closed Lemayan had his plaster off, new braces on his leg and shiny boots on his feet. He had lighter elbow crutches that made it possible for him to walk upright and proud, as a Maasai boy should walk.

His father had come by on his way home, to say that the cattle they had left for care were healthy and the warriors were busy driving them back to the village. Also, his father gladly agreed to Kemendere going home with his son. It would be good company for him when the other boys were herding. He was glad to see Lemayan so eager and happy once again. He wondered what had caused the change in that dear boy of his.

Back Home

The great day came at last. He was going home!
Lemayan was excited and went around with
Kemendere to say goodbye to the mamas, Naado
and the other white Grannies.

'We'll see you again, Lemayan,' they all said.
'You'll come back next term.' Then Naado called
Kemendere aside.

'Make sure you bring Lemayan back with you.
He is a bright boy. He would do well at school.
He seems happier these days. Here are some
shillings, for your bus-fare, soap and anything you
will need. We will be praying for you, that you'll be
a help to Lemayan and be a good witness in the
village for Jesus.'

Naado gave them a ride to town where they
would catch the bus. Arriving in the little town,
they went into a shop. Lemayan bought some
sweets, but not for himself. It would make him look
important in the eyes of the children of the village
if he had sweets to share with them. Kemendere
bought a half-kilo of sugar, with a packet of tea
tied to it, to give to Lemayan's mother. It was
the gift visitors usually brought to their hostess.
Lemayan felt sorry he had not thought of getting
something for his mother, but he was glad that
his friend had.

Kind passengers helped them put their wooden boxes on to the bus. They chatted happily, interested in everything they saw along the way, but on arrival, had a lovely surprise.

'Look! Over there!' Lemayan spotted his mother and two big sisters. He pointed them out to Kemendere excitedly. They had come all the way from home to meet them. After joyous greetings the girls took their wooden boxes to carry. They found that Kemendere's box was heavy, but when they felt how light Lemayan's was, they laughed and took some of the extra food that mother had bought and packed a lot in it. Lemayan wondered why Kemendere's box was so heavy. He must have brought his schoolbooks with him. Why carry them around? The only book Lemayan was interested in was the small black-covered book that told all about his Shepherd, Jesus. He asked his mother how she had known they were coming that day.

'Your Father asked at the Child Care Centre when he visited you there. They told him today's date,' Mother explained. 'Then when I heard that you were bringing a visitor, we came to get extra food to welcome you both. Also, we know that you males don't like carrying loads, so the girls came with me to carry your boxes,' Mother teased.

Lemayan's heart glowed afresh with love for his mother, who was always kind and thoughtful. He also grinned at the jibe about males carrying loads. True! Carrying was women and girls' work. A man, if he had to carry something heavy, would hoist it up on his shoulder. But let there be a woman handy, she would be commanded to fetch her carrying strap and take over the job. Men were made for walking in front, free to protect others from danger!

'Eeuo Lemayan! (Lemayan is back!') The children, seeing the party arriving, ran everywhere shouting excitedly, announcing his arrival. There was a grand welcome. Every one admired Lemayan's new boots, the braces on his weak leg and his shiny-new elbow crutches. He introduced Kemendere proudly to everybody.

He gained great popularity by giving each of the little ones a sweet to suck. Sweets are a great treat. They are sucked and taken out of the mouth repeatedly to examine, until hands and faces are gloriously sticky and the sweet, sadly getting smaller, at last disappears. Chewing gum is better. It lasts longer. Also, it can be shared more easily. You chew it till all the flavour is gone, and then you break off pieces and generously divide it with friends who have none.

When they were taken into his mother's house, Kemendere, as guest, solemnly gave the tea and sugar to his hostess. Mother was pleased with this polite, bigger friend her son had made, and was touched by his rather adult act.

Kemendere, on his part, was feeling sad. Lemayan had a loving father, mother, brothers, and sisters, all pleased to see him. He thought of his own family who didn't even know where he was, and didn't care. But then he remembered his Heavenly Father who loved him and cared for him, and felt comforted.

How Lemayan revelled in being home! The cattle and sheep, which had been preserved during the drought, were all back home and healthy. The ewes had lambed, so he cuddled and wanted to play with their babies all the time. The cows were in calf, so there would be milk from them soon. Some of the money from the sale of the livestock sold on that sad day nearly a year ago, was still in hand and Father had been able to buy a cow, in milk, from a neighbour.

The two boys enjoyed the smoky warm milk and also the cold sour milk – but found that their stomachs had got used to solid food. The stodgy 'ugali' Lemayan had despised before, he enjoyed now, especially as there was the delicious sour milk to wash it down.

Right from the first evening the two boys sang the songs they had learnt at the Child Care Centre and many children gathered round to listen. The tunes were of the Maasai music style and so they quickly learned them. The leader sang a line and the others echoed it. Other songs were even easier. The leader could sing any words he wanted to, and the rest would sing their basic chorus each time he paused. When it was time to chase the visiting children to their own homes, Kemendere usually prayed before they left.

One evening Lemayan's father came in and heard Kemendere's prayer. Later he asked him about it.

'Ero! (O boy!) When you prayed this evening, I heard that you prayed to Enkai the Great One, like all Maasai do.' Then he asked, 'But why did you say 'In Jesus name' at the end. Who is this 'Jesus'?'

Praying in his heart for God's help, Kemendere answered, very respectfully, 'Father of Lemayan, 'Jesus' is the name God gave to His Son when he sent him to be a man, to live on earth so that we people could know what God is like. We ask God for His blessings in the name of Jesus, because God loved His Son very much and will give us what we ask when we ask in that name.'

'Ai!' exclaimed the man, 'That is just like a tradition we Maasai had long ago. No one seems to practise it these days. It was that if a poor man was in desperate need, he had the right to go and ask a rich man for help in the name of his firstborn son. The rich man was honour bound to give that help, because of his love for his eldest son. Now you say that God has a Son and we can pray to Him in the name of that Son! That is something we Maasai can understand. Who told you about this Jesus? Why haven't we Maasai been told about God having a Son?'

'It is all written in this book.' Kemendere held up his precious little black book. 'People, who knew God's Son, Jesus, long ago when He lived on earth, wrote many things about what He said and did. This book has been translated into our language. May I read a little bit to you now?' Kemendere offered.

Being given permission, he opened to John chapter 20 verses 30-31 and read:

All these things were written in this book, to help you to believe that Jesus is the one sent by God, God's own Son. If you believe in Him you receive life of a quality that lasts forever, because of that name.

'Life that can last for ever? No my boy, that cannot be. We Maasai know that there is no such life. Life ends when the body dies. There is no kind of life that lasts. There can be no life after the body is dead,' Lemayan's father protested. 'Your book talks of things that cannot be.'

'But Father, (a boy will call any senior man Father, out of respect) we Maasai believe God gives life, don't we? If God chooses to give life of a kind that starts in this life and continues after the body dies, is He not able? Can our Life-giver not give life where He pleases?'

'Ugh, boy' he protested again. 'Your book says things new and hard to understand. These things are not for us Maasai. We have our beliefs from our fathers. We know and follow those. You school people have left the old truths.'

'Respected father, allow me to say one last thing,' Kemendere pleaded. 'We Maasai believe we are God's favourites. Would God bless people of other tribes and races with a blessing like eternal life, and refuse to give this, his biggest blessing, to his favourites?'

'True, son, God favoured the Maasai and gave us cattle. If these strange words of a life that continues after the body dies are true, we Maasai should know the secret of how to receive it. You can read to me again another day. Good night for now.' He rose; hitched up the blanket he wore, coughed and spat into the fire, bent his head to get through the low doorway and wandered off to find more adult company, who had no new disturbing ideas.

As the boys lay down, Lemayan was glad he had Kemendere with him. His friend could read the little black book. He could answer Father wisely. His last thought as he drifted off to sleep was, 'I wish I were wise like Kemendere and knew more of what is in the Bible, like he does!'

Learning to Read!

'My friend, if you had not been here last night,' Lemayan spoke to Kemendere gratefully as they wandered about the next morning, 'I wouldn't have known how to answer Father like you did. I so much want Father and Mother to believe in Jesus.'

Kemendere kept quiet. The reason why his wooden box was so heavy was that he had brought many books and papers with him. All the Nursery School books - with letters, with syllables, with easy words, with pictures to help the learner remember. He even had the Grade One readers.

Together with Mama and Naado, he had hatched a plan. He would read many things about Jesus from his New Testament, that little black book. He would keep trying to make Lemayan say that he wanted to learn to read. That might make him change his mind about going to school.

'Please read that part I like best about the Good Shepherd. Point to each word so I can see them,' Lemayan pleaded. Kemendere smiled. His young friend was getting very near to saying, 'Please teach me to read!'

After they had walked about, admiring the cattle, petting the lambs, they sat down on stones placed in the scanty shade of an acacia tree, and Kemendere opened his New Testament at John chapter ten. Lemayan gazed at the black marks on the paper. How could he ever know how to read this precious book?

Kemendere took his finger and placed it on a word at the top of the page. 'That word is 'YOHANA' – that is the name of this part of the book. What is this word?' 'YOHANA.' He turned the page and pointed to the top. 'Is this the same?'

'It seems to be.'

'Then what is that word?'

'That word says 'Yohana' (John) also! They look the same!' Lemayan soon got to recognise his first word by turning page after page and finding

YOHANA. He was excited. Perhaps he would be able to learn for himself, not just listen to his friend reading to him.

'What was that verse you learnt on your first evening at the Child Care Centre?' Kemendere asked him, knowing that he remembered well.

'Those words that Jesus said? That's easy! 'Ara nanu Olchekut Supat'. (I am the Good Shepherd.)'

With a little stem of grass Kemendere pointed down the page to a word in tiny letters, 'That word is 'ara', the next is 'nanu', then comes 'Olchekut', and this last one is 'Supat'. Show me which word is 'ara'?'

Lemayan gazed hopefully at the paper but there were so many little black marks that he couldn't find 'ara'. Kemendere pointed patiently again.

With another little grass stem, Lemayan also pointed, 'Ara nanu Olchekut', and said each word again, and again, and again – he felt wonderful. He could read!

'Oh, my good friend, please teach me to read. Let us spend every day of the time you are with me, before you go back to school, doing this. Please teach me to read this book.'

Kemendere was happy. Lemayan had asked to be taught to read. His young friend did not know how long the road was to learn to read accurately and fluently. But this was a good beginning. He still had not said he would go to school, but perhaps this taste of reading would whet his appetite.

'Let's go back to the house. There is something I want to use to teach you,' Kemendere suggested. In the semi-dark of the house, he opened his wooden box. Lemayan spied, under his few clothes, the white gleam of many papers and books. His friend selected one and they went and sat on wooden stools outside the house.

'Of course, you know how to count,' Kemendere started his lesson. 'Count one to ten for me.' Lemayan did that easily. In their games, all Maasai children learn to count, along with learning to talk.

'Now count again, using the finger signs.' Lemayan again said the numbers and proudly did the finger sign for each number. When a Maasai uses a number in conversation he always makes the sign, rather like deaf people sign with their fingers.

102

'You know counting by saying and by signing. Now you'll learn to read the numbers.'

He produced a paper with numbers up to twenty. Pointing to them in order, he read them and then told Lemayan to read them. That was easy. Then came a paper with the numbers all mixed up. That was harder, but he recognised some. For others he had to look back on the first paper. After a while they went inside for a good long drink of sour milk. Learning to read was a job that made one thirsty.

After the drink and a rest, while they chatted, Lemayan asked for another reading lesson. Kemendere handed him the book, the New Testament, open at Yohana.

'Here is a big black 1. Now find 'ten' in big black numbers. These big black numbers show us the 'ematua' (chapter).

Lemayan caught on and soon found a big 10. He was feeling very clever.

'Now go down in that place where the big 10 is and find 'eleven' in small numbers. The small numbers show the 'Ikererin' (verses).' Lemayan found that, by following the numbers, '11' appeared out of the mass of black marks.

'Now read the words that follow number eleven,' Kemendere pushed him further.

'But I can't read yet!' objected his frustrated pupil.

'But you could read those words this morning. Have you forgotten them already? Look carefully,' Kemendere goaded him on. Lemayan gazed blankly at the squiggles that meant nothing to him. Then he remembered.

'Ara nanu Olchekut Supat,' he shouted out the words. 'Now I can read my favourite verse for myself.' Kemendere took the New Testament from him, closed it and said, 'Now find it again, all by yourself.' This took time and a struggle, but when he found it, he shut the book and tried again. Soon he was finding it more easily.

By the time Lemayan could find Matayo, Mariko, Luka as well as Yohana,* and could recognise all his numbers, and find verses, he was very proud – he thought he could read!

*Matthew, Mark, Luke and John

Sharing the Good News

That evening, with Mother, Father and his bigger brothers and sisters gathered, Kemendere prepared to read another verse to them all. He handed the book to Lemayan. 'Find Yohana, then find the big three, then find the little sixteen and I will read the words.' He had set his pupil a test but he was sure he would manage it. It took a while, fumbling with the pages, and squinting in the dull firelight.

'There it is, Yohana 3:16.' He was excited and his family all beamed at him. Their young boy was learning things they themselves didn't know. Kemendere read that wonderful verse.

'For God loved the world so much, that he gave us His only trueborn Son, so that all that believe in Him, will not be lost, but will find life that endures.'

'Father of Lemayan,' he said, 'yesterday you said that we Maasai, who are Enkai's favourites, should know how to get this kind of life that does not end at death. Listen again and tell me. What did God do because He loves us?' He read the words slowly, again.

'It says, that He sent his Son. He sent His Son because He loves us,' Father answered. He had clearly understood that part. But Kemendere had another question for him.

'But how does knowing that God sent His Son help us? Why is it important to know that?' He read the verse slowly and carefully all over again.

This time it was Lemayan's mother who answered, 'It says that when we believe in Jesus, God's Son, we are given that kind of life that never ends. But why must we first believe in this Jesus, before God can give us that new life?'

Kemendere thought and then asked, 'Mother of Lemayan, if your father were on the other side of a deep, fast-flowing river and he had a gift to give you, could you receive it?' Lemayan looked at his dear mother as she thought about that question. He so much longed for her to believe in Jesus.

'No,' she answered, 'I could not receive it, unless we could find something to make a bridge that would join us.'

'Yes, and that is why we must believe in Jesus. He is our bridge. Jesus is the bridge that God has prepared for us. Sin has come between us, and God. Jesus is the one who joins us to God again, if we are willing to walk across that bridge, that is - to believe in Jesus in our hearts.'

'But what is that sin that has come between God and us people he made?' one of Lemayan's sisters asked.

'It was the Dorobo who made a noise when God had commanded silence, that time when God gave us cattle. God cut the strap that joined us to God in those days,' Lemayan's big brother said.

'Yes, that story tells us that it was disobedience that separated people from God,' Kemendere agreed. 'But there is a story in God's first book, the Old Peace Agreement, that tells us that God used to come down and talk with the first people he made. He wanted that friendship to continue. God gave them everything he had made because he loved them but he had one taboo. He showed them one fruit tree and told them never to eat the fruit of that one tree. The wife and the man ate the forbidden fruit and God counted that as sin. We also, all of us, have been disobedient to God. We have done things he forbade. We all have sin.'

'I don't!' responded Lemayan's father. 'I have never murdered, or cursed my father, or done any harmful thing to any of my age-mates. I have no sin!'

'True, honoured one,' Kemendere conceded politely. 'According to Maasai traditions you have no sin. But God tells us more in his book. Any disobedience is rebellion against him. To Enkai disobedience is the sin that separates us from him.'

Lemayan's mother could see that her husband was getting upset. He prided himself on his upright behaviour. He didn't like what he was hearing, so she hastily changed the subject.

'What then must we do? And how does believing in your Jesus bring us to God?' she asked, and Kemendere tactfully turned to her husband for his help.

'Father of Lemayan,' he asked respectfully, 'please help me here, because you know the customs of our people. When Maasai feel they are unclean in Enkai's sight, what do they do to be cleansed?'

This was safe ground for the proud man. He knew and observed the ways of his people. 'When someone is unclean through some unacceptable behaviour, he offers a sacrifice. He chooses a bullock or a sheep to be the sacrifice, but not just any one. The animal must be perfect, no sore, blindness or limp, to be accepted by God. That animal is slaughtered as an offering to God. Certain cuts of meat and the blood are given to him. This is called the 'olkipoket' – the 'cleanser.' It is considered that the animal died in the offender's place, and he is forgiven.'

'Thank you, Father,' Kemendere responded. 'Jesus, the Son of God, came to be our olkipoket.

He only, amongst all who have lived on earth, was without blemish. He obeyed his Father in every thought, word and deed. Because he is God's Son his blood has great power. It can cleanse the sins of all who accept Him as their olkipoket.' These words were met by a long thoughtful silence.

Then Lemayan's father spoke. 'These are difficult and new words. If they are true they are very good. But new things need to be thought through, chewed over, discussed by our elders – we Maasai do not readily change. You young folk change more easily, especially the ones who go away to school.' He felt insecure. He was used to reigning supreme in his family – so he changed the subject.

'What has my young son learnt to read today? Lemayan, read to us something new that you have learnt.'

Proudly, Lemayan took the New Testament, paged through nervously to find Yohana, then, a bit more confidently, he found the big black '10'and then the little '11'.

'Father, these are the first words of God's book that I learnt at the Child Care Centre. They are words that Jesus said about himself.' Then, pointing one by one to the first four words, he read, ' 'Ara nanu Olchekut Supat.' The rest of that line says, 'The Good Shepherd laid down his life for the sheep,' but I don't yet know which words are which! Father, I love those words because I have accepted Jesus to be my Shepherd. He died for me. He is my olkipoket.'

'Thank you son,' his father said quietly. Then he stood up, stretched, hitched up his blanket and said, 'I am going to arrange my trip to the cattle auction tomorrow.' He went out and everyone sat quiet, looking into the fire. Lemayan's mother broke the silence.

'Let's sing those songs you taught us yesterday, Kemendere. We want to be sure we remember them.' So they relaxed and enjoyed a good sing until the visiting children drifted off to where they slept, thoughtful and quietly happy.

As Lemayan lay down to sleep, his heart was running over with joy. Not only because he had started to learn to read God's book, but, mainly, because of the peace that Jesus had put in his heart, as he had been able to tell his parents and brothers and sisters about his new faith.

Learning is not Easy

The next day Kemendere got out more papers and books from his box. He wanted to teach his young pupil seriously. But Lemayan looked at those new things with suspicion.

'I don't want to learn those silly school books. I only need that black book, the New Testament. That's what I want to read,' he protested. But his teacher thought quickly.

'Lemayan,' he spoke gently, 'if you wanted to go to the town, could you get there without walking the path? No! Well these papers are like the path for you to walk on. Reading is like building a house. To build this house your mother went out and cut many sticks and wove them together to make the walls. Words are made up of letters. Letters are like the sticks of your mother's house. When you know them, you can put them together in new ways, to make other words.'

When he saw Lemayan looking stubborn he warned him. 'Unless you let me teach you the letters, I won't continue teaching you to read.'

'Oh, sorry!' Lemayan answered quickly. 'I thought that was just a silly school thing. I'll learn them as fast as I can so we can get back to that black book.'

So they started on 'a, e, i, o, u.' He recited them over and mixed them till he knew the sound each one said. Then they put other letters before them - 'ma, me, mi, mo, mu,' and 'na, ne ni , no, nu.' Kemendere tried to teach him so many of these funny sounds like – sa, se, si, so, su, and ka, ke, ki, ko, ku, - that he was even saying them in his dreams that night!

The next day he found out that those little bits of words, joined together, made whole words.

'Look at 'na, ne, ni, no, nu," Kemendere told him. 'Say the first and the last one. Put them together.' Lemayan struggled – na, nu. Then the light dawned.

'It says 'nanu" (meaning 'me') he said excitedly. They tried with more and more little bits, put them together and made words, until Lemayan thought he was really learning to read - till the next day came and he found he had forgotten many of the things he had learnt the day before.

When Lemayan found his head was tired and the close black lines of letters were jumping before his eyes, Kemendere gave him a treat.

'You find Luke chapter 15 verse 4, and I will read your favourite story to you.' Lemayan struggled to find the place, but it was worth all the effort as Kemendere read, slowly, pointing to each word, the story of the shepherd who went out to look for his sheep that was lost.

'Read it again!' pleaded Lemayan. He remembered the day at the 'tinka' when he had heard the voice coming out of the box, where a little black plate had spun round and round. He also remembered the 'senema' that the Grannies

112

had shown them at the Child Care Centre - the night he had called out to the Good Shepherd, Jesus, to find him. Now he was safe in His sheep pen. Then he read to them the lovely psalm about God being our Shepherd. He told them more about the Shepherd who loved each of them and wanted them to be his own sheep. When the children all went back to their homes, they were left with just Mother and a couple of big sisters, enjoying the quiet after all the noise.

'Kemendere,' Mother turned to her visitor, 'I am very, very glad that you came home with my son. You have helped him very much. But you have also opened my eyes to new things about Enkai and his Son; the words you have read to us from that black book. I want to believe these things because they are sweet to my heart, but I know so little. While you are still here with us, please help me to know more. Perhaps it will be good to do that when Lemayan's father is not home. He listens for a little while and then gets tired. His heart is not open yet. Thank you for teaching Lemayan to read. When he really knows how, he will read God's book to us. Then we will be able to learn how to follow this wonderful new Shepherd.'

So over the next few days Kemendere found many opportunities to chat to Lemayan's mother and to show her many verses in the New Testament until she too believed in Jesus and became one of His children, one of His sheep.

That Shepherd, up in heaven, was busy that very evening, calling the angels to rejoice with Him over another lost sheep that was found!

Lemayan's Big Decision

'I wish you were not leaving tomorrow,' Lemayan said longingly to his friend and teacher. 'There is so much I still have to learn!'

The two boys had had a wonderful time together. Day after day Kemendere had taught his eager pupil another verse from the precious black book. Lemayan was building up a storehouse of verses to read to himself and to share with his family, and with the children who came to sing in the evenings.

But Kemendere knew that reading was not all that easy. This was only the beginning. If only his pupil would agree to go to school and learn more. So he tried again.

'Lemayan, my friend, this matter of reading is not easy. There is much you won't be able to read when I am not there to help you. Come back with me. Learn properly, at school, every day. Learn Kiswahili and also the tongue of the white people. Then you will have many books to read and enjoy, and to share with your people here at home,' Kemendere pleaded, but he saw stubbornness growing on his young friend's face.

'No! I won't go to school! I don't want to go away! I will stay at home and learn by myself. Father promised me long ago that I would not have to go to school.' Kemendere dropped the subject – but he remembered the Grannies, Naado and the mamas at the Child Care Centre were all praying for Lemayan to change his mind. He decided to leave the answering of their prayers to Enkai Himself.

It was a sad day when Kemendere left. Mother tactfully arranged to go on a shopping trip to the trading centre where he would catch his bus. Big sisters went with them, carrying his wooden box, as he struggled along on his crutches, all singing together the new songs he had taught them.

Lemayan had been left to keep an eye on the younger children while mother and the girls were away. He felt lonely without his friend. He resented being left with the children. He was a boy. Herding was his job. Then he felt resentful about his useless leg. Also, what would he do day after day without Kemendere to teach him?

So it was a sulky, unhappy boy that his mother and sisters came back to. The young children hadn't listened to him. He missed his friend. Even the food that Mother had brought back didn't please him. The singing, praying and reading verses felt flat when it was left to him, without his bigger friend to lead it all.

'Why don't you teach us another new verse?' his younger brother asked one evening. 'Why do you just go on teaching us verses we already know?'

'I'll have a new one to teach you tomorrow,' Lemayan promised. He frantically spent the day trying to find some place in the book that he could read, some place that he could put those bits of words together to make whole words. But evening came and he had no verse to give them.

'Just let's sing this evening,' he suggested. 'I

am too tired to read tonight.' His mother guessed at his difficulty and smoothed it over. But he felt a failure. He couldn't read anything new without his teacher's help.

The next morning he tried to join in with the care of the cattle but found no place for himself. Their cattle were few these days and the warriors didn't need the help of a mere boy. He tried getting involved with the sheep, the calves, the lambs and kids – but each boy had his responsibility and wasn't for sharing his job with anyone. After all, he had been home for four weeks and had been absorbed with Kemendere and reading and had not tried to help then. Poor Lemayan found that he just wasn't needed anywhere.

Of course he didn't know of the prayers for him back at the Child Care Centre. Kemendere had told them about the good times they had had at Lemayan's home. He had told of the progress he had made in learning to read and of all the times he had shared God's word with the family. 'But Lemayan doesn't know enough yet to go on by himself. He'll forget all I taught him,' sighed Kemendere. '

So the Grannies and the Maasai mamas cried to Lemayan's Good Shepherd to bring him back to where he could learn more of reading, but especially more about Jesus. It was all these prayers that were now causing the turmoil in Lemayan's heart.

One day Lemayan wandered off, away from the village. He wanted to be alone. No, not alone, he remembered that he had a Good Shepherd, who had promised to care for him. He cried out with all his heart to his beloved Shepherd.

'Jesus, I promised to follow you and now I seem

to have got lost. What must I do? I am useless here at home. I want to read your book. Please help me! Tell me what you want me to do!' He waited to hear whether Jesus would answer with a voice from heaven. But heaven was silent.

He limped back home and went in for a drink of milk. His mother saw he was unhappy and spoke gently to him.

'My dear son, thank you for bringing Kemendere home for those four weeks. He has told us much about God's book. But he has gone. How are we to hear more? Go to school, my boy. Learn to read. Learn about the new way of your Good Shepherd and come back and tell us more.'

With that, Lemayan's dread of school melted away. School was the place where he would learn to read! Perhaps his role was to be the schoolboy of the family, to be the one who goes out and learns new things and comes back to his people to bless them with those new ideas. His Good Shepherd had answered his prayer. Not through a voice from heaven, but through his loving mother's wisdom.

That evening Mother spoke to Father. 'Your son Lemayan has something to ask you. Give him the opportunity. Make it easy to ask you. It is a very big matter for him.' He understood and they smiled.

'Father, I have something to say,' Lemayan began.

Father encouraged him. 'I'm listening, my son,' he answered gravely, guessing what was coming.

Lemayan swallowed hard. 'Father, please may I go to school? I want to go to school to learn to read properly.' His father pretended to be surprised.

'But my son, you have always hated the idea of school. You made me promise I would never send you to school. Are you asking me to break my promise?'

'But Father, you are not sending me. I am asking you to allow me to go. That is different!'

'Lemayan lai,' Father spoke kindly, 'you may go with my blessing. You have a good head and you'll learn the things of school easily. I will be proud of you. Go and become wise in the new ways, and lead our people in understanding those ways in the future. Just as you put your heart into our beloved cattle, go to school and put all your heart into it. But never forget, you are a Maasai. You will always be a Maasai.'

His Second Home

'There's Lemayan!' The shout rang out from the gang of boys kicking a ball around on the field. They had paused idly to watch as the bus stopped and they recognised him struggling down. They rushed across the field, hopping, swinging or limping. This time he was not shy - he was back among friends!

Chief of the welcoming committee was Kemendere, smiling broadly. Lemayan was led triumphantly to the kitchen. When the mamas saw him, there was a chorus of 'Meisisi Yesu' (Praise Jesus). A boy was sent to give the news to the Grannies in their house nearby. They all bustled over to welcome the 'lost sheep' and they too greeted him with 'Meisisi Olaitoriani (Praise the Lord).

'Why are they so happy to see me?' a bewildered Lemayan asked Kemendere. 'I wasn't very nice when I was here before.'

'They have all been praying you would come back, and that you would agree to go to school. I told them about the good progress you had made in learning to read. They are happy that God has answered their prayers. You have come back to stay now, haven't you?' he added anxiously. 'You have changed your mind about school, I hope?'

'My Good Shepherd has changed my mind for me, Kemendere. I tried to go on learning. I failed. I could not find any new verses to read to my family. I asked God to help me. I didn't know what to do. He used my mother to help change my mind, and suddenly I agreed with my whole heart that I would come back here and learn properly in school. You should have seen the surprise on my father's face when I went and asked his permission to go to school.' They had a good laugh. 'But he was glad and sent me with his blessing,' he added.

Lemayan was happy. Back in the dormitory he was surprised to find his pyjamas and sheets neatly folded in his locker, patiently awaiting his return. These people must have great faith in God when they pray to Him. They had really expected him to come back!

But there was one uncomfortable thought worrying him. Schooling always started with Nursery School. Would he be put with the four- and five-year-olds? He cried out in his heart, 'Jesus, please let me go to 'big school'. Nursery School is no place for a nearly eight-year-old! I don't want to waste time with the babies!'

At supper Kemendere had hopeful news for him. 'Naado has told me to take you to school tomorrow morning to ask the Headmaster if he will accept you into Class 1, without first going to the nursery classes. I will tell him about your learning at home in the holidays.' God was answering his prayers so quickly! The two boys spent the evening together practising, A,B,C.... and 1,2,3.... and ma, me, mi, mo, mu, and all the other things the Headmaster might test him on.

'No, I am sorry. It is a rule of the Education Department. I must have your report from your Nursery School to file with your admission form.' The Headmaster was very firm in his refusal the next morning, as they shivered in his office. Kemendere plucked up courage to fight for his friend.

'But Sir,' he protested politely, 'this boy already knows all the things the children learn in Nursery School. He knows his letters, all the numbers, even further than little children learn. He knows all the syllables, and can read lots of things.'

'Can he write?' The Headmaster asked and the two boys looked at each other in dismay. They had been so keen on reading that they had completely forgotten about writing! They scuttled out of the Headmaster's office defeated, but Kemendere had a plan.

'Go back to the Nursery School. Ask the teacher to show you everything that the children have to know to pass into Class 1. She is very nice. You will spend only one day in her school. Then you'll have Saturday and Sunday to learn how to write those letters you already know. On Monday morning we can show her what you have been writing. Then she can say in the letter that you qualify to start big school.'

His plan worked. The Nursery School teacher didn't want a big, nearly eight-year-old know-all in her class of little ones. On Saturday, when the two boys had finished their duties, they went to sit by themselves at a table in the dining room and settled to the task of Lemayan's writing. First came the figures 1-10. That didn't take long. Next came letters, syllables and words. Kemendere insisted that everything he wrote must touch the line it was standing on. That took practice.

They were both glad when the lunch bell rang and they could stop for a while. Lemayan was left alone after lunch, writing carefully, getting the letters and numbers all standing on the line, and exactly the right shape. Later Kemendere came and began teaching him to write the capital letters. That was harder. They all had to stand with their feet on the line, but their heads had to reach the line above also. His hand was tired and his head over-full.

'Let's go and play football now!' Kemendere suggested. Lemayan hesitated.

'I don't know how. I've always called it a silly game. The other boys will laugh at me,' he started making excuses. But Kemendere persisted.

'None of us knew how to play this game when we started. We tried to kick the ball and lost our balance and fell over. We all laughed at each other's efforts but slowly we managed to kick without falling. It is much more fun than doing the dull exercises the mamas do with us to make our legs stronger.' Then Kemendere gave his friend a final push. 'Of course if you don't want to play because you are scared, you can go inside and do exercises with the girls!'

Lemayan swallowed his bait. 'I'm not scared! I won't go and do exercise with the girls. Of course I'll play. It was just that I don't know if I can.'

Soon he was in the fray, kicking and missing, falling and laughing, and learning to use his crutches to keep his balance. He also quickly learnt that a crutch was very useful – it gave you another, longer, 'leg' to stop the ball! He was now a real schoolboy – he played football.

There were other fun-things to play. Later, as he

settled into life at his new home he enjoyed them all. There were tricycles to play on – hopefully to make their weak legs strong. Some of the boys were clever. They put their useless legs over the handlebars and bent down to peddle with their hands. There were other things like bicycles that had no wheels. They sat on chairs and turned the pedals, as fast as they could. There were also swings. The boys of his age despised those because the mamas would not let them swing very high. Lemayan wanted to go on those swings because they were still new to him, but he was afraid the other boys would laugh at him.

There was another big wooden structure they had great fun on. Lemayan loved climbing up the steps, then sitting on the top and sliding down. It was even more fun going down with his friends, three or four together, ending with a wonderful mixed-up-tumble at the bottom. No one got hurt and they all laughed a lot. He was surprised to find that he enjoyed the games at the Child Care Centre even more than the games at home.

But all that came later. He was now still desperately trying his best to know the things that Headmaster might ask him on Monday.

On Sunday he went to church. Every time the Pastor said, 'Let us pray,' Lemayan switched off from what the Pastor was saying and prayed very desperately his own heartfelt prayer. 'Lord, please make that Headmaster accept me in big school. Please help me to remember everything I have been learning. Help my hand form those letters and numbers neatly, and make them all stand nicely on their lines.'

His prayer was answered. The Nursery Teacher wrote a letter praising all Lemayan's abilities. The Headmaster, still doubtful, told him to write his name. He looked at Kemendere in alarm – he had never written his name! But Kemendere smiled at him encouragingly.

'You can do it. Write le – ma – yan, and make a capital 'L' at the beginning.' He did it, to his own and the Headmaster's surprise.

'Kemendere,' the Headmaster turned to him, 'you are a good teacher. I hope one day you will be able to attend Teacher Training College. Today your first pupil has passed his test well.'

'Lemayan,' he said smiling, 'you may go to Class 1. You are a clever boy to have learnt so well and so quickly. Go, and work hard!' The two boys scuttled out of the office triumphantly and soon Lemayan was seated in the classroom, getting welcoming smiles from his friends.

How proud he was when, at the end of the morning, the teacher called him and gave him books – some to write in, some to read, some to do things with numbers in. She told him to write his name carefully on each cover. Concentrating hard, biting his tongue and, clutching his pencil tightly, he wrote:

'Lemayan ole Lenana' - and so started the many years of his education.

New Lessons Learnt

Life at his new home became one long adventure. He was learning many things every day. One good thing he learnt was not to feel sorry for himself. Many of the others in the Child Care Centre had far bigger troubles than he had.

There was Maanda, who was blind. He had been a strong healthy bright boy, proud of his herding skills, as Lemayan himself had been. Then he got measles, which left him completely blind in both eyes. Those Flying Doctor nurses had found him, as they had found Lemayan, during one of their clinics and had brought him to the Child Care Centre to go to school. He was puzzled, how Maanda could learn to read if his eyes were blind. That truly must be a miracle!

Lemayan was surprised to find out that there was, at the boys' school, a teacher for the blind who himself was blind. He was of a different tribe so he didn't know the 'enkutuk oo Lmaa' - the mouth of the Maasai, which was the only language Maanda knew. Yet somehow they communicated because soon Maanda was skilfully feeling with his fingers along the lines of raised dots in his books and reading out loud what those dots said. At first he didn't understand what he was reading – he just said the sounds his fingers told him. As he learnt to speak and understand English, the sounds his fingers felt, started to make sense. Lemayan admired him. He walked with confidence. He was always smiling, and was a very responsible boy and always very clean. By the time he was in Class 4 the mamas entrusted him with the keys for locking up at night – his sensitive fingers could easily tell him which key locked which door.

There were also deaf children at the school. About six deaf boys attended a special school on the far side of Nairobi. Some of them had become deaf in a meningitis epidemic. Their parents brought them to the Child Care Centre at the beginning of each school term and Naado took them to their school and fetched them back for the holidays. Lemayan watched them. He was glad to be able to see and hear. He was thankful.

One day Lemayan was walking behind a new boy, struggling to walk on crutches on his recently straightened legs.

'Ashe Yesu! Ashe Yesu!' Parsaluni was saying, 'Thank you Jesus', with each wobbly step. Lemayan drew level with him.

'Why were you thanking Jesus?' Lemayan challenged him.

Parsaluni smiled. 'Because, for the first time in my life I am walking. I had polio when I was very small. My granny carried me on her back everywhere. She even carried me when I got old enough to attend Nursery School. Then when I was too big to be carried, my father bought a wheelbarrow, and the other schoolboys wheeled me to school on it every day. Now my legs have been straightened and with these irons and boots, and with the help of these crutches I am walking! No more wheelbarrow for me!'

Lemayan was ashamed. He had enjoyed his childhood, running freely. He had proudly taken his place as a herder of his father's sheep and calves. He had never been humiliated by being carried or wheeled around like a sack of potatoes. When he got polio, only one leg was affected. Yet he had grumbled and felt sorry for himself.

Then there was little Njaa who was brought to the 'Enkaji oo Nkera.' – a young girl who couldn't even sit, much less stand. Only her legs were paralysed, but her back and arms were weak from not being used. Lemayan watched with caring interest as her treatment started. Naado was determined that Njaa would walk. A leather corset helped her to sit. Operations straightened her legs. Braces could keep her legs straight. The mamas and Naado spent hours doing exercises with her, trying to spark any possible movement in her weak limbs. But they despaired of those little stick arms. Would they ever be able to handle crutches? Njaa persevered bravely. Then one day she surprised Naado.

'Look, Naado!' she exclaimed excitedly. She flexed her little skinny arm, squeezed her fist, and pointed proudly to a tiny ping-pong-ball-sized biceps rising faintly on it. This was duly admired and all were spurred on to continue with the weary hours of exercising.

One day Naado challenged her. 'Njaa, no one is going to carry you to Nursery School today. You are going to walk. I'll walk just behind you. I'll catch you if you fall. You can rest against me if you get tired. I don't mind how long it takes to get there but I am not going to carry you, even the last little bit of the way!'

It took a very long 40 minutes to shuffle the 50 yards down the concrete path to the classroom.

It cost lots of tears – Njaa's tears of tiredness and frustration, and Naado's tears of sympathy for her and of resisting the temptation to give up and carry her. But the clapping and cheers of the children when they arrived at the classroom door quickly wiped the tears away and brought smiles to both of them. The next day it took only 20 minutes. As her strength and confidence increased the time got shorter, and eventually she could walk there at a fair speed with no one to nurse her along the way. But she wasn't satisfied for long.

'Naado,' she demanded, 'I want to go to the big school. These children in Nursery School are babies. I want to go to real school with the other girls of our dormitory.'

'Yes Njaa,' Naado answered, much to Njaa's surprise, 'certainly you may go to school. It is a long way, but you can do it.' It was only about two hundred yards but far for Njaa. 'But you must first learn one thing. Here, when you fall you always lie and cry till someone picks you up. You may go to school when you can get up by yourself when you fall. Big school doesn't want crying babies.' Njaa thought that was cruel, but was determined to do it. Naado also thought it cruel, but she had to make Njaa independent.

The next few weeks saw a strange sight - a little crippled girl walking a few yards, then letting go of her crutches and falling. Then she would gather her crutches to her, position them and struggle up, only to do this over and over again. At first others hurried to her aid, but she refused help. One day she felt she was ready to face the hoards of active girls rushing around at big school.

'I am ready, Naado. Look!' she called. Then, dropping her crutches, she fell. Naado winced, as she had often done when she had peeped through the window at Njaa's brave efforts. She longed to pick her up, dust her down and give her a hug. But she resisted and watched the brave struggle.

'Right, I'll take you tomorrow. No, not to help you,' she added hastily as she saw a stubborn look on Njaa's face. 'I'll go with you to the Headmistress to tell her that you are strong enough and also to take the Nursery School teacher's very good report of you.'

It was a proud day for Njaa, walking to school, having her name written down as a schoolgirl, going into the classroom and becoming one with the girls of her age. But for a long time she didn't walk with the other girls in the mornings. She set off a good ten minutes before the others, to leave time for falling! She was never late.

One day Lemayan got the shock of his life. A Maasai man brought his son to Naado's office. The boy, he noticed, walked well and looked strong and healthy. He was not crippled, so Lemayan wondered what his trouble was. Then he caught sight of his face. There was a great split between his mouth and his nose, and teeth stuck out at all the wrong places. Lemayan was shocked. He had never seen this before. He tried to imagine what it must be like for that young boy. There and then Lamayan decided that he would never again feel sorry for himself. His disability was so small in comparison to that of others. He didn't live in darkness or silence. He wasn't weak like Njaa nor been carried in a wheelbarrow like Parsaluni. He didn't have to worry about the way he looked.

And he hadn't been thrown out by his family as Kemendere had been.

'Ashe Yesu' Lemayan whispered under his blankets that night. 'Thank you for your blessings. Thank you for a strong body and good head. Thank you for my eyes and ears. Thank you for my family who love me. Thank you for the people here who care for me and gave me my crutches and braces and boots. Thank you that I am in school and that I can now read that precious black book, the New Testament. Thank you most of all, that you are my Good Shepherd, and that I am your sheep. Help me to follow you forever. I will never again feel sorry for myself….' he murmured as he drifted off to sleep.

Then one day, some months later, he saw a miracle. A blanketed man and his son were walking across the playing field. According to the manners of his people, he went to bow his head to the man in greeting. Then he recognised the boy and gazed at him in wonder. The boy with the split face was now handsome and smiling with joy. Later Lemayan heard that the Flying Doctor ladies had taken him to a good children's hospital in Nairobi, that there he had had three operations to correct his upper lip and the hole in his mouth – and this was the wonderful, unbelievable result!

'Yes, my boy,' the man said, understanding his wonder, 'that is how I gazed at him when I went to fetch him from the hospital. I thought at first that they were giving me the wrong boy! Supat Enkai! - God is good!'

'Yes, that is true,' thought Lemayan. 'God is good, and he has been good to me too!'

His School Years

Happy now to be in school Lemayan worked eagerly. He found the work in class came easily to him. After half a year he was promoted to Class 2. Even there he learned too quickly, and then got into mischief, so he was promoted again and still came top of the class at the end of the year. But as he learnt English and discovered the wealth of books in the class library-cupboard, he no longer joked around in class. Whenever he got bored with what the teacher was saying, he put a library book on his lap so that he could read what interested him more.

The long years at school learning, punctuated with happy holidays back home, slipped by quickly. He often enjoyed having Kemendere with him at home during the school holidays. But after two years his friend went away to High School and Lemayan started choosing different friends. He discovered other worlds, new ideas and un-thought-of ways of living. He had always considered that being a Maasai and having cattle was the best, most satisfying life. New ways started beckoning. Instead of inviting a friend to go home with him, he went to their homes. The children at the Child Care Centre were all Maasai, but at the school there were boys of other tribes - people who grew crops, who owned shops, drove

motor cars and lived in brick houses in towns. He was dazzled by these new ways of life, feeling uncomfortable about the simple life-style of the Maasai.

The more he learnt of those ways the less he thought about the Good Shepherd whom he had come to love as a younger boy. Other books became much more interesting and up to date than the little black book so dear to him before. Back home, his family found he was not as eager as he had been before, to teach them songs and read to them from his New Testament. Instead he boasted of the things he had seen and done – all of no interest to them, leaving them feeling he had become an uncomfortable stranger.

Back at the Child Care Centre, with Kemendere, away at High School, the boys grew rebellious. He was no longer there to keep the boys obedient and respectful to the Mamas by his good example. They started thinking it was clever to be cheeky. They felt very grown-up when they managed to find some cigarette-butts to smoke behind the classrooms at break time.

By the time he was thirteen years old and in his final year in primary school, Lemayan was irked by the discipline of the Child Care Centre. It made him impatient to be with so many smaller children. He was looking forward to the time when he would leave this stuffy religious place, go away to high school in the big city and really start to live it up.

Registering for the public exams at the end of primary school, all pupils are required to write the names of the three high schools of their choice, with the hopes of being selected for one. Lemayan, being sure that his marks would be high, confidently chose the three most prestigious boarding schools in the country – and spent exam time in happy dreams of his fancy future, while many of his classmates wrote, knowing that they had no hopes of anything greater than the shoemaking course given to crippled boys.

One day Naado called him. 'We have some good news for you. Your sponsor overseas, hearing that you are doing very well in school, has offered to carry on paying your school fees after you leave here.' She explained. Lemayan had been so taken up in his flighty dreams that he had not even wondered how his father would be able to pay for the expensive future he was planning.

Since the drought, when he was young, the family cattle had been increasing, but very slowly. He knew Father would not be able to give him all that the lifestyle he was planning demanded. Now, with this news, he no longer had worries – the world was at his feet.

By this time, with much exercising and practice, Lemayan had been able to discard one crutch. He could now walk proudly, but still with a limp. He liked to wear long trousers so that no one saw his brace. He felt he was ready to meet the world.

Exams over, he was impatient with all the class parties, the farewells at the Child Care Centre and especially the annual Christmas Play. He had enjoyed this play when he had been younger. It was fun being shepherds, dressed up in bedspreads and towels, or even sheep covered with fluffy blankets. Last year he had acted a very fierce and cruel Herod and had been much admired.

He now went around politely saying goodbyes to the Grannies and the Mamas, using the Christian words that he knew would please them. He suffered all their promises to pray for him, and the good advice showered on him in love. He was impatient to be away - away from restraints of the Mamas values and the high hopes of the Grannies. He wanted to be far away at a city school. He planned to throw off the old life of Maasai ways and join the modern youth of the new Kenya.

He went home to patiently await the results of the exams but found that he didn't have enough of the needed patience!

Taking the Wrong Road

Lemayan was bored. His family, whom he had always loved and respected, seemed dull and out-of-date. The cattle, once the delight and pride of his heart, no longer interested him. The wide skies, the vast plain, the dry rustling grass and scattered acacia thorn-trees – once his cradle and home, now were empty and unattractive to his changed tastes. He craved excitement, noise and loud music. He endured it at home for one short week.

'Father, please give me some money,' Lemayan asked at the end of that week. 'I need to go to the trading centre where mother does the shopping. I want to find out when the exam results are likely to be out. The date will be announced on the radio, but how will I hear in this backwoods faraway place? I need some money so that I can stay there for a few days waiting for news.'

'Yes son,' Father smiled at him, 'I know how important those results are to you. At the next cattle auction we will go to sell that black steer over there, to be ready with the money you will need for all the clothes and books required. It is good that your sponsor overseas will pay your fees. Our cattle are still few, but I will do what I can to provide what you need.'

'Son,' he added seriously, 'what are you planning to do with all this education you are getting? Don't forget your people. Study well the things that would help us. We suffer in drought. We lose cattle to East Coast fever. Our grazing is sparse. Come back and help us care well for the cattle Enkai entrusted to us.'

'Oh yes, Father. Of course I'll come back,' Lemayan answered glibly. But his heart was planning another lifestyle that didn't include cow-dung huts and skinny cattle.

Later in the day his father called him. 'Son, here is some money for a few days stay in the town. Also, a neighbour came yesterday to pay me cash for two goats he bought from me recently. So I am giving you that money to go and pay a debt I have at the Indian's shop.' Lemayan accepted the responsibility gladly. Father did not add any more instructions – he had always been a reliable, honest boy. Why insult him with warnings of being trustworthy?

Lemayan was glad to get away from home. Everyone there expected him to be the boy he had been in years past. The dingy town had little to offer, but at least he was free to do as he pleased! He hung around a disco the first evening. He revelled in the loud, wild music, but he wasn't allowed in, being under age. He couldn't dance anyway with that crippled leg of his. The next day he just mooched around and palled up with four idle youths. They caught him drinking a coke and demanded that he buy cokes for them all.

Then he remembered the debt Father had asked him to settle. He hurried towards the shop, before his newfound friends could finish off his money. He was a bit uncomfortable with them. They were older and more worldly-wise than he. He was beginning to realise how young and ignorant he was of the life that he was aiming at entering.

On his way he saw a man listening to a radio. 'Excuse me sir,' he asked politely, 'have you heard on the radio the date that the Primary School results are to be published? I am waiting for my results, but I live miles away, in the bush.'

'No,' the man answered, 'there is no report yet. You had better buy one of these little battery radios. Then you can tune in wherever you are and hear for yourself.' What a temptation! That money was burning a hole in his pocket, crying out to be spent! Not only for his exam results. He would be in touch with that tempting world waiting out there for him!

'Where could I buy one? How much do they cost?' He was hooked. He ran into the shop indicated and bought a dear little radio at the first price quoted to him. Poor Lemayan had not learnt

enough about this new world of smart people, to know that he should spend a good few minutes bargaining and getting the goods for about half the quoted price! He bought the batteries needed, learnt how to work it and spent the rest of the afternoon sitting in the shade of a tree listening to anything and everything he could tune into.

The next day he found his way to the shop to settle Father's debt. Although he was feeling very uncomfortable inside, lies were flowing freely from his unaccustomed tongue.

'My Father sent money for his debt. But he says he is sorry it is a hundred shillings short. The man who bought the goats has not yet brought all the money he owes. Father says he will bring it when he comes to town again.' He cringed to think what would happen when Father found out what he had done. But that was some time in the future. Now he had the radio. He'd have to tell another lie! He would tell his father that a friend had lent it to him, till the results came out!

He stayed a few more days in the trading centre, but it wasn't as exciting as he had expected. He went back home and listened to his radio till everyone at home was tired of the noise. Then the batteries died. The exam results were still not out. His radio was silent but he couldn't silence his conscience. He was very unhappy.

Everything Spoilt

When, one day he heard that his mother was planning to go to the town to buy supplies he was alarmed. What if the shopkeeper asked about the hundred shillings still owed? He couldn't dare let his parents find out! So one lie led to another.

In his desperation he hatched a plan. 'Father, please would you give me a goat to sell. There will be many things I'll need to buy when the results come out. I'd like to go and see what things I can get at the local shops.' Lemayan thought he had worked out a way to clear that debt before Father found out.

'Certainly, my son, you may go and select one out of your own flock.' Lemayan looked puzzled. He had no flock of his own! When his father saw his puzzlement, he explained.

'Let me tell you about what I have been doing. When I saw how well you were doing in school I decided to build up a herd for you. Every kid that our goats have produced during these last two years is yours - yours to sell wisely to provide for your needs. You said that your sponsor overseas is willing to pay your fees. You are a lucky boy, as I would not have been able to provide fees for those big expensive schools. When you hear the results I will sell that steer to pay for your initial expenses, but after that, clothes and bus-fare, pens and those school things, you can buy yourself, as you need. Don't waste those goats. I know I can trust you. There are twenty-four goats. Eleven of them are females. Don't ever sell one of those. Their offspring should keep the herd growing and keep you in pocket money till you finish school.'

Lemayan was speechless! His father had lovingly planned for his future. His father trusted him! He should have been happy, grateful and bubbling over with thanks to him. But he was desperately ashamed. If he had been a girl he would have cried, but a nearly-fourteen-year-old Maasai boy could not cry. He looked at his puzzled father with shame and sorrow written plainly on his face.

'Father,' he started haltingly, 'don't give me those goats! I don't deserve your trust. I cheated you. I lied to you!' He poured out the whole sorry tale - the temptation to get the radio, to steal the money and then to cap the stealing with a lie. 'I was asking you now for a goat,' he continued shamefacedly, 'so that I could pay the debt, and then I planned to lie to you about the price of the goat. I am sorry, Father, very, very sorry. I know I can't expect you to forgive me. Now you know what I have done, I know I cannot expect any help from you with more schooling"

'Be quiet boy, leave me! Go away!' spluttered his shocked father. 'Your words have hurt. My son, of whom I was proud, in whom I had hope. My son, who has always been honest, honourable, now stooping to cowardly lies! I trusted you, boy, and you have betrayed my trust! You are worse than a Dorobo!' (This forest-dwelling hidden people were mistakenly suspected of being deceitful, simply because they were retiring and secretive.)

Lemayan walked bleakly out of the homestead, out on to the arid plain, which was as dry and dull as his aching heart. It would have been easier if his father had been angry, if he had ranted and raged and abused him. But his father had loved him, had been proud of him, had trusted him - and now all that was lost. He wandered about purposelessly. He longed to pray but felt he had no right. He had sinned. He had long since strayed from the Good Shepherd and gone his own way.

As darkness fell, he slunk back home and hesitantly entered his mother's house. Mother greeted him solemnly. He refused an offer of food. It would stick in his throat, but agreed to sip a mug of hot well-sugared tea. He sat in the half-light of the house – but the gloom of his heart was darker. The cooking-fire in the centre of the house was turning to ashes – mirroring the ashes of his hopes for the future. Nothing was left for him. He now resented the useless leg in irons, the clumsy boot and the crutch he relied on for getting about. But for them, he could go back to the cattle, back to his first love. But for his stealing and lying, he would now be eagerly awaiting his selection to one of the top High Schools in the country. He was sure his father would not help him, and he felt he would find it hard to accept his help, even if he gave it.

Thoughts tumbled around in his aching head. He would go back to the Child Care Centre and add to his lies. He would tell the easy-to-deceive Grannies that his father had refused him help because he was a Christian – they would fall for it and give him everything he needed. But more lies wouldn't ease the shame and ache in his heart.

His mother at last got through to him. 'My dear boy, your father has told me everything and he is angry now. But just be quiet and respectful and I am sure in a few days he will change. Son, I too am shocked – to cheat your father is a grave thing to a Maasai. Our people, as you know, think it is clever to cheat 'ilmeek" (non-Maasai) 'but cheating your father is a very serious sin and needs atonement. Soon your father will accept what I pointed out to him, that you showed true Maasai courage when you confessed to him what you had done. Cowards run away from trouble. You faced him bravely. Go and look through the herd he has for you and choose a perfect goat. Be ready for when he changes towards you. I will tell him you are prepared to offer the needed olkipoket (cleansing sacrifice) Just wait humbly till he is ready.'

Lemayan felt a little uncomfortable with the talk of olkipoket. He had learnt that Jesus, the Good Shepherd is our cleansing sacrifice. That 'He had laid down his life for the sheep'. But he was far from that Good Shepherd now. He had drifted away and then deliberately turned further away. The days passed and he no longer had any desire to hear the long-awaited exam results. He would not be going to high school, whatever his results might be.

Into all this gloom, two young schoolboys from the trading centre came running, to bring the good news that the results were out. His marks were very high, and he had been selected for entrance into Alliance Boys High - in the opinion of many, the top school of the country. They had found Lemayan's father outside the village, so he had received the news first.

He slowly absorbed this gratifying information. His son, his own born son, chosen for the top school of the country! His crippled son whom many pitied, chosen above hundreds in the land! He opened his blanket and gave a little self-congratulatory spit on a string of blue beads on his chest, as is the custom when an elder is unexpectedly lucky or is feeling pleased with himself.

'Find Lemayan,' he ordered the excited boys. 'Tell him to come to me here immediately.' They scuttled off to find the hero and were rather disappointed at his reception of the good news. Lemayan hurried off to obey his father's call, with fear, while the news-bearers went all around, telling everyone their puzzling message. They knew little of exam results and high schools, and even less about something called 'high marks'.

Lemayan stood before his father, respectfully, with his head bowed. 'I have come Father, you called me.' He wondered dully what his father's response to the news would be.

'Son, I have heard the news of your success at school. I am proud that you did well. The other matter we will forget. You did right to tell me and not hide your 'eng'oki,' (a weighty word for sin, meaning deep guilt). You have felt your shame. Your mother has told me you were prepared to offer the olkipoket. I think you have learnt your lesson. I'll give you that black steer over there.' He pointed to the animal he had previously selected for sale. 'Your brother may go tomorrow with you to drive it to the butcher. We can't wait for the cattle auction. Those two schoolboys, who came to call you, can help you drive a few of your goats as well. Sell them, settle that debt and buy what you need. I will sell no more cattle for you. If you spend wisely – no more useless radios – the goats will see you through.'

Lemayan was overwhelmed. He felt a huge burden of guilt and uselessness slide off him. He tried to thank his father but he roughly quietened him and strode off. Lemayan hurried back to his mother's house, his mind reeling, his excitement rising. From hopelessness, to the sudden fulfilling of all his dreams in one moment, was just too much to take in. He sat silently trying to plan, trying to think clearly. His mother understood. She called the two schoolboys in for some refreshment, and they chattered happily while they ate, and while Lemayan picked idly at his food, in a dream.

By the next morning he seemed to be the old Lemayan again - eager, happy, making plans and saying goodbyes. He would sell the animals, and go with the money to the Child Care Centre. His letter from the High School would be waiting for him there, with a list of all he needed to buy - school uniform, other clothes, shoes, socks, jersey, pens, a good geometry set, soap, shoe polish - the list was endless. The letter would also tell the amount of money he would need to take to school for textbooks and stationery. Naado would give him a cheque for his fees, a gift from his sponsor.

The next few days were a blur of activity. More goodbyes, selling goats, bargaining, excited

greetings back at the Child Care Centre, more choosing and buying. The Grannies even took him to Nairobi to buy the things not available at the local shops. Then on the day of registration, Naado proudly took him, as his guardian, to the city to get him registered at Alliance Boys' High School. He should have been happy. He soon made friends with two other Maasai boys. He liked the school, the studies, the food, everything – but deep in his heart he was miserable. He didn't recognise the real reason. He was, in truth, lonely for his Good Shepherd. He felt guilty, grumpy, and out of touch. He thought it was homesickness. And in truth it was of course a form of homesickness – for his Friend and Saviour, Jesus and for his Father God, the great Enkai, who had blessed the Maasai people with their beloved cattle.

At Peace once More

'Excellent work, Lemayan,' the teacher said when he returned the first essay of the year to the new boys.

Right from the start, in the classroom, Lemayan shone. His hand shot up quickly when questions were asked. Almost every time the teachers returned essays or other assignments, his came back to him with some word of praise. The work was challenging but he studied hard and enjoyed it.

Yet out of the classroom he was miserable. During his Primary School years, when he had been with other disabled children, he had never felt handicapped. But here all was different. Strangers in the school wrote him off as 'that crippled boy' and despised him. His friends felt sorry for him – which was almost worse. At lunchtime they would rush off for a strenuous game of squash or tennis. After school they all donned their games-kits and ran off for soccer, hockey or rugby. He never mentioned that he had played football when he was younger. They would laugh uproariously at his version of soccer – all hopping and swinging on their crutches. Free time was a lonely time for Lemayan.

'We're going over to the girls' school. Want to come with us?'

The first time his friends invited him on this jaunt he accepted gladly. They gave 'needing to see their sisters' as the reason for going. Other times they went without asking for permission. They all had sisters or cousins to visit, but usually were more interested in the other boy's sister than in their own! Lemayan hobbled there that first time, slowing down his friends on the way. But the girls, catching sight of his crutch and his ungainly raised-boot, showed no interest and left him out of the banter and teasing that was the order of the day.

Girls and sport were the constant subjects of the other boys' chatter. He felt included only when someone needed help with a maths problem, or wanted some chemistry mystery explained.

He could easily be welcomed and included in the breaking of school rules enjoyed by of some of the boys. Sometimes smuggling in of tins of beer, smoking the odd packets of cigarettes, or even some experimenting with drugs, seemed fun at first. The danger of being caught by the staff added excitement to the doubtful enjoyment of these forbidden activities. But on the whole, Lemayan wasn't attracted to the boys who did these things. And when their conversation descended to boasting of girl friends, he pulled out of those activities too.

But when he discovered the riches of the library he no longer found time hanging heavy on his hands. He spent long hours of real pleasure there. There were books on every subject, more than he could have imagined. But he was still lonely. Then one day this loneliness ended.

'Hullo!' A tall smiling student addressed him. 'I don't know your name. I guess you are a new boy in Form 1. I often see you reading here in the library.'

Lemayan was happy to chat. 'I am Lemayan ole Lenana, a new Form 1 boy, from Kajiado District. Yes, I come here most days during sports time. My paralysed leg doesn't let me play sport. This is a terrific library. My primary school just had a small cupboard that they called a library. What's your name?'

'I am Kamau, son of Njoroge, from Nyeri District. I am in Form 4, writing my finals this year. I have given up sports for a while. I need to study hard so that I get a good pass.' They chatted a while, having a laugh about the rural schools where they had started their education. They enjoyed comparing backgrounds – Kamau from the fertile agricultural highlands, and Lemayan from the dry, vast grazing lands of the southern plains. He felt flattered by the attention of this senior student, and was warmed by his friendliness.

'By the way,' Kamau said as they parted, 'some of us meet for a Bible Study most evenings, after supper and before prep time. We meet in a room at the back of the Physics laboratory. You'd be welcome any time to join us if you would like to.'

Bible Study! Lemayan remembered how he had loved his little black book - the book that had started him reading. He remembered the first verse he had read for himself. 'I am the Good Shepherd, the Good Shepherd laid down his life for his sheep.' That night, lying in bed, remembering those days when he had loved his Bible, and loved the Author of that book, he felt a strange mixture of loneliness and comfort – loneliness because of the loss of his Friend, comfort in the thought that maybe, some time, somehow, he would find Him again.

'Hullo Lemayan!' It was Kamau who spotted him as they were streaming out of the dining hall after supper one evening a week later. 'I'm on my way to that Bible Study I told you about. How about coming with me to meet the others.'

Lemayan was glad. He had several times tried to pluck up courage to accept the invitation. But he was shy. What if they were all senior students – they might not want a mere Form 1 boy joining them. He had felt rejection from so many students here already. He didn't want to risk another. But going with his new friend was a different matter.

'Sure, I'll be glad to come along with you!' he responded, and was hustled down the lengthy veranda and round to the room where the Bible Study group was gathering. He was impressed by how many there were, all hurrying in, and at the friendliness of those who noticed him following Kamau. They sang a few rousing choruses, one boy led in prayer and then they all got out Bibles. There was also another book. Lemayan took a peep at the one in the hand of the boy next to him – it was called 'Studies in the Gospel of John – work book'.

When they settled down, Kamau stood up. He was evidently the leader. He welcomed everyone and said that if there were new members they could buy the workbook from him before next week. Lemayan was glad not to be welcomed by name because he was not sure he was going to join.

Kamau continued, 'You will remember that we had finished chapter 9 and we are going to start today studying John chapter 10.' Lemayan gasped! The Gospel of John, chapter 10. His own special Good Shepherd chapter! Surely God Himself had brought him to this Bible Study. Perhaps his Good Shepherd still knew about him and still loved him!

He drank in all that was said. Questions were discussed. One boy gave his testimony of how the Good Shepherd had found him when he was lost. Another spoke of how this Good Shepherd had cared for him and helped and led him through a time of trouble. They discussed the matter of 'other sheep' and several asked prayer for friends that they were hoping to introduce to the Good Shepherd.

Lemayan's heart was filled with longing for that joy and sense of belonging that he had had as a young boy, before he got proud and drifted away. Would the Good Shepherd come and look for him – like in that story he had first heard on that little black plate on the box that talked his language. He decided to come to Bible Study every evening.

'There will be no Bible Study next week,' Kamau announced. 'We will meet as usual but it will be for prayer. On next Saturday evening some Christian brothers in Nairobi are bringing the 'Jesus Film' to our school. We want to pray that all the boys will come to see it. We want to pray that many will find salvation in Jesus through that film. Start praying now! Start inviting your classmates,' he exhorted them.

Lemayan was disappointed. Just when he had decided to join, they stop. He didn't want to come to pray. He didn't pray any more. God was too far away. He was even hearing in Science classes that all the talk about God having made the world was out of date. No one believed that these days. Some were even saying that believing in God was out of date.

But he would go to see the film. He remembered the filmstrip pictures that those Grannies had shown them long ago. He remembered crying when he had seen the picture of Jesus on the cross. What a pity, he felt, that he had left those things behind, as he grew older. How awful it would be if there truly were no God!

Lemayan's friends didn't seem interested in the film. They had seen plenty of films. They didn't need a religious one. But when the great evening came, his two Maasai classmates agreed to go with him. The film was enthralling. Things he had heard at the Child Care Centre came back to him. Even his favourite story of the lost sheep was in the film. As he heard the sheep bleating in fear, Lemayan felt he was that sheep, lost, in the dark, far from his Shepherd.

He closed his eyes when the soldiers beat Jesus cruelly. He could not look. But when all was quiet and he opened his eyes, there was Jesus on the cross. He seemed to be looking straight at him.

His heart melted. Tears flowed freely. He was glad it was dark and no one could see. 'There is my Good Shepherd dying for me. He loves me. He still loves me. He is looking for me. He wants me back.' These and many other thoughts tumbled around in Lemayan's mind. But most important was his prayer – 'Jesus, please find me again. Thank you for dying for my sin. Forgive me for straying away. Keep me. Hold me, all the days of my life. I am yours, with all my heart. I love you.'

'How did you like it?' Lemayan asked his two friends as they went back to their dormitory. He hoped to make an opening to tell them what had happened in his life during that wonderful film. He remembered the glorious pictures of the come-to-life Jesus and knew He was alive and with him.

'Mm. It makes one think,' one said quietly. 'If all that is really true, it must be very important to believe it.' That was just the opening Lemayan wanted.

'It is true and it is important.' And he went on to tell them how he had believed as a little boy, of the joy and blessing of that faith. How he had drifted away, and not asked forgiveness. How this evening he had come back, been forgiven and restored, and was determined to follow Jesus, whatever the cost. Little did Lemayan guess what the cost would be in keeping that promise! His friends didn't comment as they went into the dormitory and straight to bed. He lay with a joyous feeling of, once again, being loved and accepted.

In the coming days he attended the Bible Studies and made many friends among the Christians. He asked permission to go into the city to buy a Bible. To his delight he found a beautiful bright red Maasai Bible – the whole Bible, just newly published, not only the New Testament he had had as a child.

He felt burdened about his Maasai classmates. He tried to interest them. Several times he told them of some helpful verse he had found in the Maasai Bible. They showed mild interest but were both very noncommittal. Then one day he found out why they were hedging.

'During these coming school holidays our sub-tribe is holding our 'enkipaata.' We want to get all those ceremonies over, after that we'll give this Christian thing a hearing. We are not going to miss these important ceremonies.'

Lemayan understood. The 'enkipaata' was the huge ceremony for the 'cleansing of the boys' - hundreds of boys, to prepare them for their initiation, their passing from boyhood to warrior status – the pride of every Maasai. But Lemayan now realised that he could no longer be part of those ceremonies. The 'oloiboni' or prophet, claimed to be the bridge to God. Lemayan remembered the verse he had learnt long ago.

'Jesus said, I am the way, the Truth and the Life, no one comes to the Father except though me.'

Sacrifices of a flawless lamb are made at those cleansing ceremonies. And Lemayan again remembered a verse learnt long ago, when John the Baptist said about Jesus:

'Look, there's the Lamb of God, that takes away the sin of the whole world.'

He realised then that a big test of his faith was lying before him, and cried to his Good Shepherd to hold him true and faithful to Himself.

His New World Tested

Lemayan remembered the fun he had had, as a younger boy, as he had counted the days to the school holidays - the joyous anticipation of going home. Holidays! Freedom from bells! Long drinks of delicious smoky sour-milk! Home!

Since he had come back to his Shepherd, the rebellion in his heart had faded. He no longer wanted the bright lights and the fast life. He once again appreciated the security, the love and the values of home.

But today, on his way to his home village, he worried. Perhaps the enkipaata was being arranged in his area also. Hopefully it would only take place when he was safely at school again.

As he walked the miles from the bus to his home, he had time to think and pray. No one met him any longer. He now had a back-bag so that he could carry everything himself. He noticed that there had been good rains. The grass was green and lush. The bushes had new green shoots. The livestock would be healthy and milk abundant.

He realised that these were exactly the signs, which showed that he was in danger. Ceremonies such as the enkipaata were arranged only if milk was plentiful, the livestock sleek and the grazing available nearby.

As he arrived at the home village he knew just what lay ahead. There was a buzz of many people, of much activity, of getting prepared for something big. Children came running out to welcome him home with excitement.

'Suba Lemayan! Ieuo?' (Greetings, have you come?) The children crowded round him chattering.

'Yes, I have come!' he answered laughing. 'What's all the excitement about?

'People are all coming for the enkipaata, they explained. Everyone is busy with brewing the beer and preparing everything else. Your father asked them to wait till you arrived. He was not sure when your school was closing but he hoped you would come soon. He will be so glad to see you!' Lemayan's heart sank. His father had taken it for granted he would want to be part of this ceremony. He knew that his son had long-since left following his once-loved Good Shepherd. How would he make his father understand? Every Maasai boy normally longed for this ceremony, this celebration of the beginning of his growing up.

'Lemayan lai!' His mother came out her house and greeted him with joy. How dear she was to him. Perhaps she would understand. Chatting together, 'eating the news' as it is called, Lemayan discovered that his father had gone to the chief's village but would be returning that night. Good. At least he would be able to explain his case later to his father in the quiet of their home.

He spent the afternoon wandering about, greeting, chatting with his friends from near and far. He didn't mention the ceremonies, he just told of school, of Nairobi and other news. Deep in his heart he was crying to God for help. He made sure he was safely in his mother's house before dark – to be ready when Father came.

'Ng'sak, Papai!' (Here I am to be greeted, Father) Lemayan rose as his father arrived, and bowed to present his head for greetings. He remembered that if he were to enter into the ceremonies now being planned, he would no longer greet adults in this way of a child. He would be a man, greeting adults as an adult.

'My boy,' his father started speaking eagerly, 'I'm so glad you have arrived. I have persuaded the elders to wait for you to come home. Now you are home the enkipaata can start without delay.'

Lemayan looked bleakly at his father, knowing how much he was going to hurt him. 'Father, I am sorry, but I am not joining this enkipaata.' He tried to speak gently and respectfully, but he knew full well his father would be very angry.

'Father, I have chosen another way. The way God's Book shows us. I don't need the enkipaata for 'cleansing'. The blood of Jesus, the Son of Enkai has already washed me. I don't need the olkipoket to die for my sins; Jesus died on the cross, and my sins have all been forgiven.' He hoped Father would understand.

But his father was scarcely listening. All he heard was that Lemayan was refusing the traditions of his people. That he was not going to join in this ancient ceremony that gathered the boys of the present to be the next generation, the elders of the future. The more he heard and thought about it the angrier he became.

'Silence!' he shouted. 'You obey me, or get out! Unless you join in the enkipaata you leave this home and never return. You will no longer be a son of mine!'

Lemayan's mother tried to protest, but to no effect. 'Quiet, woman. Do you want a son who disgraces us? A son who will never take his place honourably as a man amongst men? I can't stay in this house tonight. I will sleep elsewhere. Try and talk some sense into this idiot son of yours who has lost his way. He must leave this village in the morning and never return, unless he comes to his senses.'

Lemayan scarcely slept that night. He loved his Saviour and wanted to please Him. He also loved his father, his mother and his home dearly. Where would he go? What would he do if he were chased from his home? As he prayed, peace came to his heart. He didn't know how this crisis would be resolved but he knew that it was in the loving hands of his Good Shepherd.

By morning Father had lost his anger and hoped deeply that Lemayan had relented. He loved this clever son of his. He hoped they could make peace. He was glad when he saw Lemayan approaching him. They greeted solemnly.

'Yes my son, what have you to say this morning? Has the new day brought new sense?' he asked hopefully. How Lemayan hated to hurt his father.

'My Father, whom I respect and love, I have come to say goodbye, sadly, but at your command,' Lemayan said, with sorrow but firmness in his voice.

His father blustered and tried to argue, tried to talk him out of his decision. He could not believe that his dear son would leave his home, his parents, all that he loved, simply for a belief in a book!

'Father, I have always obeyed you. I love you and Mother, my home and my people. But I have someone over me greater than you. As a Christian I obey what God teaches in his book. God Himself, through sending his Son into this world, has made His way for us to be cleansed. How can I go for the oloiboni's blessing? God's book teaches that He has given us the only one who opens the way to Him – that is Jesus Christ His Son and Him alone.'

Father was speechless. This wasn't a young boy's rebelliousness. His son was speaking respectfully, from the depths of his heart. This was a deep conviction that was so important to his son to follow, that he was ready to leave all he held dear. This was not insubordination, but obedience to God Himself. How could he, his earthly father, force him to do what the great God did not want of those who followed the ways taught in His Book? His heart melted as he looked again at his brave son.

'My son,' he said gently, after a pause, 'if these beliefs are so important to you that you are willing to leave your parents and your home for them, then I have no right to force you to go against what you believe. God's authority is greater than mine. You are brave. In that at least you are a true Maasai. You may stay, and may your Jesus bless you.'

They parted quickly. Tears were threatening in the emotion of the moment. Father strode off to an elders' gathering and Lemayan scuttled into Mother's dark, welcoming house, to share the good news.

What rejoicing there was between Lemayan and his dear mother! He told her all about his wandering, his loneliness, and then seeing the film, seeing his Good Shepherd dying on the Cross to save His wandering sheep. He told of his frustration and friendlessness at school - and how all that had been washed away when his Friend, the Good Shepherd, Jesus, had come back into his life.

'My dear boy,' his mother said with tears in her eyes, 'when you and Kemendere told us these words about Jesus, God's Son, long ago, I believed in Him. I wanted to follow Him. But when you changed I thought that you had discovered that the words in that little black book of yours were not true. So I went back to the old ways. But I have often thought of those verses from the Bible that you taught us when you were a child. I longed for them to be true. Please pray with me now. I want to come back and follow Jesus with all my heart.'

The angels in heaven must, once again, have been leaning over the walls of heaven rejoicing in the lost sheep coming back into the fold. Jesus was very present in that dark smoky cow-dung house – fulfilling His promise, 'Where two or, three are gathered I am there'. Jesus Himself made the third!

And from that day on, when Lemayan's mother went out in the morning to start the milking, instead of praying to the morning star, she prayed to the God who had made that star. Instead of offering the customary little splash of milk, she offered herself afresh for that day. Life was new and wonderful.

New Help for Lemayan

'Father,' Lemayan approached his father gently, 'I feel it would be easier for you if I was not at home during the enkipaata celebrations. So may I go to visit my friends at my other home – the Child Care Centre?' His father was relieved and gladly let him go.

Getting off the bus he remembered the first time he had arrived at the Enkaji oo Nkera, as he had called it then – how the boys had rushed out to escort him in, and all the new things that had come into his life.

He remembered the second time, when he had decided voluntarily to go to school because he wanted to learn to read the Bible. Now he was coming back, a big boy, and a different boy.

One of the Mamas recognised him striding over the field and came out to welcome him. They 'ate the news' for a while. Then Mama gave her big news.

'Naado and Daniel have just returned from Korea. They went there to learn more about helping those who have had polio. Run over to her house now. They will all be so glad to see you. The Grannies are visiting her to hear all their adventures in that far-off land.'

He remembered Daniel the shoemaker, also crippled by polio, who had always mended the children's boots and the leather straps of their leg-irons. What had he gone all the way to Korea for?

Lemayan got a big welcome. There was great rejoicing when he told of his meeting again with his Good Shepherd, of his big test and how God had heard his prayer and softened his father's heart.

'I have good news for you, Lemayan,' Naado said, and he wondered what it could be. She went on telling him about things they had learnt in Korea and the ways crippled legs could be helped.

'This is where you come in, Lemayan,' Naado continued. 'I have often seen your father in the past and I remember that he is a very tall man. If you grow to be his height, your strong leg will be very much longer than your weak one. You would need to have a very large, clumsy raise on your boot. But we hear that a surgeon could operate on the growing-ends of the bones of your good knee to stop those bones growing further. Then your legs will not be too different in length. You are a good height now, tall enough. What do you think about that?'

Poor Lemayan didn't know what to think! He would love to be taller. Maasai take great pride in their height. But each time his boots had worn out he had needed a bigger raise. Truly he would not want one any bigger than the one he had then.

'Think about it, Lemayan. I don't need an answer today.' Naado saw his struggle, but had further, easier news. 'But there is something Daniel could do for you today. Let him tell you himself.'

Daniel beamed his lovely smile. 'Yes Lemayan, I am no longer just a shoemaker, I have learnt metal-work and now make the leg-irons myself. In Korea we learnt about lighter aluminium ones that also have a hinge at the knee. I could measure you for one and possibly by tomorrow or the next day you could be wearing a lighter brace. It has a little lever that you open when you sit down so that your leg can bend, and you close it when you stand up, to keep the leg straight.'

Lemayan didn't need to hesitate to reply to this good news! 'Wonderful!' he exclaimed. 'Let's go to your workshop right now. You can measure me immediately. As I get bigger it is embarrassing to have my leg stiff – sticking out like a sore thumb!' They all chuckled at his leg being likened to his thumb, but all agreed about the difficulty, and the help the knee-hinge would be.

Naado had further news. 'Perhaps there is still more that can be done!' she told him. 'We have seen people in Korea who have had an operation, transferring the tendon on the side of the knee, and attaching it to the kneecap. With exercises, that muscle can then control the knee movement, and then you would need only a small brace for your ankle. If you persevered with exercises you could walk without a crutch and, possibly without a limp.'

Lemayan sat with his mouth open, amazed at the possibilities! Just a small brace well hidden under his trousers! No crutch and no limp! He would be almost normal! Truly it was God Himself who had brought him to these dear people again. Had he not come back to his Good Shepherd, he would never have heard of all these wonderful

helps. He would have been in the enkipaata
activities. All the other boys would be pitying
or despising him for not being able to jump.
Learning to jump was a big thing in the enkipaata
time. When the boys became warriors, jumping

(as well as lion hunting) was the pride of every one. But his friend, Jesus, had rescued him. Truly, he was well named Lemayan – the blessed one.

So by the time he went back to school he had a new brace that could bend at the knee. How different to sit in the bus, or at his desk, with his knee bent. He looked forward to the time he would be able to throw away his crutch also.

One holiday, during the next year, Lemayan had the muscle transplant operation. After the weeks of exercises under Naado's strict supervision, he was able to leave his crutch behind when he went back to school. He still had a limp now and then, and his hand often went to his thigh to help him climb a step. He knew that if he persevered with his exercises eventually his walking would be normal. Truly God was good to him.

When Lemayan was 16 years old Naado took him to see a surgeon in Nairobi who decided that it was unwise to let his good leg grow any longer. He went in to hospital in Nairobi for the operation to stop his good leg growing. He had a happy time recuperating at the Child Care Centre, staying with Daniel. He marvelled at the skills Daniel had acquired on his second trip to Korea. While Lemayan was with him, he was busy making a little false-leg for a girl who had been rescued from a crocodile's jaws - but had lost a leg.

Daniel was himself badly crippled but nothing could be done for his condition because he was already adult when all this help became known. How grateful Lemayan was for being found while he was young, and for all who had helped him. He remembered too the family overseas who sent a cheque regularly for his school fees – he wrote often to them and was never ashamed to send his school report which they required.

During the years at High School, his friends were mostly of the Bible Study group. He threw himself into all the Christian Union activities. He invited and chatted to others in his form and gradually one and another joined him in his stand for Jesus. Studies still came easily to him. He usually came first in his form. He passed well, year by year, with several subject prizes, into the next Form. Missing sport and girlfriends was no longer a hurt. He was whole inside, and even becoming whole in body, as more and more ways of overcoming his disability were found.

The Light Spreads

School holidays brought varied adventures. During some he went with friends of the school Christian Union to hold campaigns in their hometowns. He loved preaching and he wondered whether he would become a minister in the future!

One special vacation time in his final year, Lemayan visited the Grannies. He was received with joy, but they were even happier as they heard the reason for his visit.

'My Grandmothers,' he smiled at them, 'I want some of the evangelists you are training for the four weeks of the school holidays, to come home with me to preach in my village, and all the villages round about. I have tried to tell people about Jesus, but they say that the message I bring them is for the educated who have got lost to the old beliefs of our people. They will listen to your evangelists more than to me, a school boy.'

The Grannies were very happy about what he wanted to do. 'Yes,' Ng'oto Ntoyie said, 'I am sure some of them would be glad to go. There are thirty of them here now for a teaching course and tomorrow, our closing day, we will be making plans for their work for the next few weeks. Come tomorrow morning when the bell rings for our praise and prayer session. You can have a chance to speak to them. Give them your testimony and then put in your request. We can then see which of them would like to take the light of the Gospel to your area.

Two days later his request was answered. Four eager evangelists were bundling up blankets and clothes, and the food the Grannies had given them to take to the hostesses in the homes where they would stay, on this 'missionary journey'. These men were eager to share the news about Jesus with their fellow Maasai. None of them had been to school as children. They were all typical Maasai young men, yet, as adults, they had met Jesus and He had changed their lives. The Grannies had gathered the first few, then others like them, taught them to read, and then regularly called them back for 2-week teaching sessions so that they would have some 'meat' in their preaching. After that they all went out in twos or threes to Maasai villages, where people had never heard of Jesus.

When all the bundles of blankets and clothes, along with cartons of provisions and big cans of water, were safely tied on the roof carrier of the Land Cruiser, they paused for prayer, asking God to use them in blessing in Lemayan's home area. Then the Grannies, Lemayan and the four preachers hopped in eagerly, and drove off to the farewells and good wishes of all the others.

As they drove smoothly down the main road, Lemayan wondered with dread about the part of the journey ahead when they would leave the tarmac. No vehicle had ever gone right to his home village. There were several cattle paths leading to Tinga where the borehole was. There was a footpath formed by people coming to shop at the trading centre. But this Land Cruiser was far wider than the people walking single file on the narrow path. He looked anxiously at Ng'oto Ntoyie who was driving, and felt she was rather old for such a task.

They stopped for mandasis and Coke at the trading centre and then started down the footpath. They wove back and forth between the thorny trees, getting scratches and scrapes on the poor vehicle. They rode right over small bushes in the way, and through muddy puddles. They all kept their eyes open for ant-bear holes and for stumps hidden in the grass. Once, crossing a sandy riverbed, they nearly got stuck. As the back wheels started spinning, digging into the soft sand, Ng'oto Nyoyie changed into 4-wheel drive, low ratio gears. Lemayan was amazed at the power of the Land Cruiser as it, as if by magic, climbed up out of the hole it had dug and 'walked' as surely and slowly as a tortoise, across the sand and up the far bank. By the time they reached his home village he had greater respect for the battered vehicle and its elderly driver than he had had when they started.

What a joy it was for him to have the Grannies in his home, drinking tea with his mother and chatting with his father. Kokoo Lmurran quickly made friends with the children. She surreptitiously gave two cute toddlers a sweet and in no time hoards of children appeared from nowhere, just to be around while sweets were given out. Then Kokoo heard one child coughing, got her little medicine box out and gave her a spoonful of cough syrup. After that everyone coughed! Lemayan's mother wisely came to the rescue and sorted out the genuine coughers from the hope-for-syrup coughers. The mothers clamoured for eye medicine and the grannies for liniment for their sore backs.

Later Lemayan climbed up on the Land Cruiser and tossed the bundles to those waiting to help, handed the cartons of food down carefully, and handled the big cans of water even more carefully. Everyone wanted the visitors to come and stay with them, but were satisfied when they understood that these men were staying for 4 weeks, so that all would have their turn. Hospitality, to the Maasai, is a joy. However little they may have, strangers, provided they were of the right tribe, were always welcome and given the best.

The two Grannies were eager to start for home and asked Lemayan's father if a man would accompany them to the main road in case they got lost. One man gladly climbed in, just for the novelty of a ride, but everyone was puzzled. Why should these elderly ladies need a guide? Could they not see the 'footprints' of the 'legs' of the car? Would they not recognise the trees, rocks, hills they had passed only this morning. They decided it must be because the driver was a woman!

Once the vehicle had gone, the four men divided their loads, and were taken by eager hostesses, one to each of the four nearest villages. Children carried smaller things, women and big girls tied their skin straps round the water cans and heavy cartons, swung them on to their backs and all set off happily, singing the choruses Kemendere had taught them long ago. Lemayan and boys of his village accompanied the visitors to introduce them to the headman of each village and see them settled.

The Light Spreads

That evening in each village, in crowded smoky houses or outside in the moonlight, the evangelists gathered the women and children and sang, talked of Jesus, the Son of Enkai the Creator, and prayed His blessing on their homes. Elders don't sit with their children and wives in public meetings. After the 'children' had had their fill, the men gathered and asked questions and chatted with the preachers. Some argued, some doubted, some listened with great interest, others drifted off.

But all were surprised and impressed by one thing. These preachers had never been to school. They had never been spoilt by the new ways of education. They were full Maasai, had been through all the steps of growing up. They each had the usual holes in their earlobes, and the customary lower front teeth removed – yet they were different - changed, free, happy, friendly men. When they were asked, their answer was always, 'Yes, I was like you. But when I believed in Jesus he changed me. Jesus, God's Son took my sins, forgave me and came to live in me to make me new.'

This went on for three weeks. During the day they tramped together to further villages to share the good news of Jesus. In the evenings they separated, each in the village they were assigned to, telling more and more of the new Way they themselves were following. Some young people, women and even a few men were serious about wanting to join this new way, to believe in Jesus and become changed people. Much time was spent with them, teaching the Christian life and how to follow Jesus.

One day the chief of the whole area sent a message asking Lemayan to bring the visitors to his home. He wanted to talk to them. Lemayan was worried. Was the chief cross about the changes the preachers were causing? Did he want to tell them to leave, to stop bothering them with the new ways they were introducing. Perhaps the chief would want to give them honey beer to drink in his home. The preachers would not drink the beer and he might feel insulted.

But the chief had a big surprise for them all. Over huge mugs of sour milk that all enjoyed, he thanked them for coming and for the words they had brought. Then he said,

'What will we do here after you all leave? Even Lemayan will go back to school. Who is going to go on teaching and guiding us in this new life? In other areas Maasai are starting church meetings on Sundays. I have seen, in other places, Maasai people meeting under a shady tree, to sing and pray and worship Enkai and read from His book. What plans do you have for us?'

Lemayan and his four visitors were overwhelmed with praise to God, but had no ready answer to the chief's request. They thanked the chief for his welcome and then all discussed the possibilities for a long time. At last, together they made a plan.

The next Sunday, the Grannies were coming to fetch the four men, for their next teaching-course due to start on the following day. Lemayan also was due back at his school. On that day they would all 'plant' their church!

The chief promised to call the people from the eight nearby villages. They were to bring short 'ng'apeta' (strong sticks with a fork at the top) and 'ilpitoi' (long pliable sticks) as well as a good supply of strips of thin green bark the women used in building their houses. These would be used to fashion 'church pews' – rough benches planted in the ground under a shady acacia tree that they would choose in a central place. That would then become 'church'.

He ordered each village to contribute a goat for a feast and the chief himself promised to supply a sack of rice. Lemayan's mother was to arrange for women of her village to do the cooking; the women of the other villages were to bring water and firewood. The older men grumbled a bit when they discovered that no beer would be brewed for his feast. Lemayan's father arranged for many crates of Coca Cola and Fanta to be piled on to the Land Cruiser when the Grannies passed through the trading centre. Continuous all-day cooking of tea would also slake their thirst.

The last few days before the big Sunday, were busy. Women and big girls went far off onto the plains in search of the right kind of stumps for the church pew legs, the wood that termites would not chew. They brought the long straight sticks needed and carefully stripped off the bark, putting it all to soak in water to stay supple. Great piles of firewood were being stacked behind Lemayan's mother's house.

The men generally didn't do much, except quarrel about who was to donate a goat, and who was to slaughter them. They were reluctant to part with a goat, but eager to do the slaughtering – the prize was to eat the kidneys raw and still warm. The chief wisely decreed that the donor of the goat slaughtered it, and so got the kidneys! – The men all laughed at the wisdom of their chief.

Lemayan marvelled that the whole community was looking forward to the great day and most playing their part gladly. Everybody loves a feast, a celebration. This was to be the beginning of their very own church. Even those who didn't know what a church was, or who hadn't enjoyed the preaching and singing that had been going on in the past weeks, were happy to enter in to all the activities. Lemayan spent his time running around in a happy daze, trying to help everyone. He could scarcely believe what was happening. He remembered Kemendere's visit years ago, before he had started school. The verses and songs his friend had taught were still remembered. The seed he had sown was now bearing fruit.

Everything was ready by the time the villages settled down to sleep on the Saturday night. The goats were slaughtered and the carcasses hung high up in a tree, hopefully well away from leopards. A group of women had enjoyed a good chatter as they carefully cleaned the rice of weevils, stones and rice-husks. Tomorrow was the big day. Lemayan was too excited to sleep!

The Best Day of his Life

'Lemayan! Find me a sharp knife.'

'Lemayan! Where must I leave my water can?'

'Lemayan! Ask your mother for her big plastic basin.'

He was at the beck and call of everyone and was thoroughly enjoying himself. Activity had begun before daylight. Women from the further villages trickled in to leave their cans of precious water at Lemayan's home. Men came to take down the carcasses of the goats they had slaughtered and skinned, to quarter them and divide what was to be roasted (men's work) and to cut up what was to be stewed (women's work). The innards were tossed into the big plastic basin to be 'milked' of their contents and washed thoroughly. The women who were to do the cooking knew they would not get to eat any of the roast – that was men's food. Nor would they see much of the stew they cooked – visiting women and the children would consume most of that, served on large helpings of rice. But once the crowds were satisfied they would enjoy the delicious tripe, and perhaps even have some over for their families for the next day.

Outside the village, under the spreading acacia tree, willing helpers were cutting the dry grass and little bushy plants growing in the shade of the church site. Big girls made brooms of the twigs they had cut, and swept the debris away. The chief, with Lemayan's father and the four preachers, paced up and down and backwards and forwards, deciding where the legs of the pews should be planted.

'Lemayan! Cut some 'incheito' (pegs) for us quickly,' his father called out. Several boys came to help him and in no time, using the long sticks the women had brought, Lemayan produced a handful of strong well-sharpened pegs for the men. His team of boys kept cutting and sharpening more pegs, as required. The men hammered them into the ground with heavy stones, in the places they had marked. The chief, using his authority, ordered the people about and soon everyone was working. Men got out their swords, always kept strapped to their left sides, and cut the 'ng'apeta' to the required length for the legs. The women

then planted them firmly into the holes they had dug. Women all have short iron bars they use for digging holes when building their houses. The more experienced evangelists anxiously tried to supervise the planting of the legs, so that all four were equal in height, with the forks facing the right way – a sloping, uneven bench would be uncomfortable to sit on! It might even collapse!

The women were skilled in constructing the seats. They often wove little tables and shelves in their homes. They chose two long strong sticks, placed them over the forks on the legs and tied them firmly with long strips of wet bark. They tied short sticks across to make the ends of the bench, and, placing many of the long sticks side by side, they created the seat, weaving the bark skilfully in and out to keep them flat and firmly together. Lemayan admired their work but thought sadly that, with the drying out of those sticks over the coming months, they would get brittle and break and they would have to do all that work over again.

Suddenly all activity stopped! Their keen ears picked up the unusual sound of a vehicle grinding its way towards them. The Grannies were arriving.

'There are two cars coming!' Some argued about that, but, as the sound drew nearer, all could hear distinctly, two different 'voices' – then the excitement exploded as the old green Land Cruiser appeared through the trees, closely followed by a sturdy grey Land Rover.

'Naado has come too!' Lemayan shouted. 'That is the Land Rover of the Child Care Centre!' In the Land Rover, with Naado, were the two Mamas who had cared for Lemayan in all those years he attended primary school. Lemayan's cup was full.

Lemayan proudly introduced the Grannies, Naado and the Mamas to the chief and elders, and happy greetings were given all round. When Ng'oto Ntoyie expressed her admiration for the benches being made, everyone went back to their tasks, eager to show off their skills.

As all the houses of the village were filled with women cooking large pots of rice and stew, Lemayan's mother brought a big enamelled teapot out, followed by a little girl with mugs hanging from every finger. The visitors sat down very gingerly on the newly made, untried benches and found them strong and safe. They, with the chief and a few elders, were all given tea to drink, while they chatted and 'ate the news.' The visitors were very happy as the chief gave good reports of the work of the evangelists and of the response of the people to their message.

'So, this you see here, is the beginning of our new church,' the chief explained proudly.

'I have instructed all the people of the eight villages in this area to come this morning. I feel that this is not only the planting of a few benches for us to sit on, but the planting of a seed that will bring great changes in our whole community.'

As the bench making, the cooking and roasting went on, people from the farther villages started arriving. Teapots and mugs were brought out from all the houses of Lemayan's home village, and all who arrived drank the sweet, milky tea gratefully. The men then stood around little groups talking, women chatted as they rested in the sparse shade of nearby trees, children ran around, excited, casting uncertain glances at the white people. The children of Lemayan's village, remembering the sweets they had received a few weeks before, kept watchful eyes on the Granny with the white hair, hoping for a repeat performance.

Then Lemayan had a good idea. He called all the children, led them off away from the village and practised singing some of the choruses they knew. When he felt that most people had arrived, he led them back in procession, singing and clapping as they came to where the benches were. Just before they ran out of songs to sing, they noticed the Granny with the white hair going to her car and emerging with a packet in her hand. The faces and hands of the small ones were soon sticky, but all the children, and old cronies who insisted on being given one too, enjoyed their sweets and decided that this thing called 'kanisa' (church) was a good thing.

The men of the villages had a problem. It was the custom for men to sit on stools and women and children to sit on the ground. Here the men refused to sit with the women on the new benches. So they solved the problem by sending the children to nearby houses to gather their three-legged stools and leaking water tins – any thing that could be sat on. Naado produced a wooden form from the Land Rover for the chief, Lemayan's father and the evangelists to sit on, marking the front of the church.

So it turned out that the men all sat behind the preachers. The women and bigger children crowded onto the new pews and the smaller children sat, played and rolled on the dusty ground. They soon turned grey as the dust clung to the stickiness of the sweets. The three white ladies were glad of their little folding stools, always carried in their vehicles for such a time as this. They were grateful not to be adding to the weight on one of the already overloaded benches!

As the men were used to having a say in any gathering of elders, they didn't leave all the talking to the evangelists, who tried in vain to follow an order of service. Women are not used to being in a meeting where one person speaks while others listen. So some chattered and passed remarks, or called out to their children to stop doing whatever they might be doing. The chief, who knew a bit more of the outside world, explained at length that everyone should be quiet because the visitors, black and white, had a message from Enkai for them – and all knew that God should be listened to.

So silence fell on the crowd, babies and toddlers went to sleep on mothers' laps. Soon the silence was not that imposed on them by the chief, but a breathless silence as the evangelists told of how their lives had been changed as they met Jesus, the Son of the Great Enkai. The need for salvation was strongly stated. The way of entering this new life was carefully explained. Also the changes that would, or should come with accepting this wonderful new way, were spelt out clearly. They stressed that all this was a gift from God, greater by far than that of the cattle that God had given the Maasai at the beginning of time.

When the last preacher finished he asked for those who wanted to accept the offered new way, to stand up. The women and children all stood up as a body. They agreed, but how much did they understand? Not a man stirred. The preacher turned and addressed them politely, 'And what about you?'

'Oh! We believe too, we all believe. Of course no one refuses God's message,' they replied glibly.

So, at least, the community accepted having the church in its midst. The people, without anyone objecting, agreed that this message was worth thinking about. This was a big step forward and the one-by-one believing would come as they heard more.

The chief made the last speech of the day. He addressed it to the white visitors and the evangelists.

'Thank you for bringing this good message from God. Thank you for all that you have done for Lemayan, a son of this community. But what I want to ask you is this. What are we to do next Sunday, and the next? Who will tell us more of this new way?' Of course he said much more, because speeches are never short, but that was the most notable point.

While the missionaries were still thinking up an answer, Sankale, the most senior of the evangelists there, stood up. 'If my teachers agree, I will stay when the others go back tonight. When they have finished their two-week course, they will arrange for other evangelists to come. We will try to help you until you have leaders of your own. On the other days, that are not Sunday, I will visit your homes and explain more of this message.' The whole congregation clapped their excited thanks.

Naado then asked to be given a chance to say something. She said that she had noticed one child who was badly knock-kneed. She explained that at the Child Care Centre that could be cured. She asked if there were other children who had deformities of any kind. There was such a babble of answers that the chief told the people to go and talk to Naado at her Land Rover when the service was over. Sankale closed the meeting in a long prayer, praying for the people and their new church that the Lord would keep and bless them.

The first church service had come to an end. But Lemayan's big day was not yet over. There was still much more to come.

The Big Celebration

The best, of course, was the feast.

Women and children drifted off, leaving the pews for the men, who would, of course, be served first. A line of girls emerged from a nearby house carrying large teapots, full of water, not tea! Lemayan got busy guiding the girls in the washing of hands. Each girl went shyly to where the men were sitting and bowed their heads to be greeted. Then they solemnly poured a little water over their outstretched hands. Each man after that sat with his hands in front of him, touching nothing, until the hunks of roasted meat were served, handed round on large tin trays. This was washed down with Coca Cola, to the disgust of some – children's beer they called it! Then they tucked in to plates of rice with goat stew, and eventually belched loudly to announce that they were satisfied.

Lemayan was excited when his father called him.

'Run and tell your mother that I'm bringing the three Grannies and the Mamas to eat in our house. Tell her to get ready very quickly.'

He ran and helped his mother to serve rice and stew sufficient for her guests, into medium sized pots, and then to take the enormous 'suffurias' to the next-door house to continue to be served to the many women and children now on the pews, waiting. She quickly removed the debris of mass cooking, tidied up, put coloured cloths on the ends of the alcove beds for the guests to sit on, carefully washed her newest enamelled mugs, tied a pretty cloth over her shoulders and was ready - teapot and rice pot keeping warm on the hot stones that made the fireplace. The stew was bubbling gently on the fire and bottles of Fanta were being kept as cool as possible between two wet sacks.

'What a joy it is to have all of you in my home,' Lemayan's mother said as she led them in and seated them round her hearth. 'My son speaks often about you with love. My husband and I are very grateful for all you have done for him.' She enlarged on the many blessings that had come through them – care, clothes, schooling, all that had been done to lessen his disability, but most of all of the message of the Gospel of Jesus that had blessed Lemayan and come to her also. She told of how Kemendere had first helped her believe in her Saviour. She continued, 'Thank you also now for sending the evangelists. These past four weeks have transformed our whole community. And now we have a church. I'll have other believers to meet with.' She kept on talking enthusiastically, plying them with food, a Fanta to drink, more food and large mugs of smoky, very sweet, scalding tea.

Naado slipped out with Lemayan and found hopeful mothers waiting at the Land Rover. The knock-kneed boy was old enough to go to the Child Care Centre without his mother. A little girl, terrified of Naado, had a horrible burn scar under her chin that made it impossible for her to lift her head. Naado decided to take her and mother, and look for a hospital in Nairobi that could help her. Then there was a tiny baby born with clubfeet. Naado was glad she had been found so young as it would be quite easy to straighten those little feet. They could also accompany her.

'I know of a boy who crawls on his knees because both his legs are weak,' said one mother. 'His home is far but I know where he lives.'

'There is a blind boy at my brother's village. Is there help for blind children?'

'I know of a little girl who was born with a split on her lip and a horrible hole in her mouth. She nearly died as a baby because she couldn't suck on her mother. She is very thin and weak, ' another added.

Lemayan carefully wrote down the family names of these children. Naado asked him to call the chief, who then promised to send the message very widely to bring any children with any physical disabilities on the day when Sankale was to leave and another evangelist brought to help the new church. Lemayan marvelled at how much blessing was beginning to come to his home area.

As it would be a moonlit night, people from the further villages were invited to come when it was dark, to see the filmstrips the missionaries were planning to show. But long before the time, many gathered round to sing the songs the evangelists had taught them in the past four weeks. Naado produced a player and the little records that talk Maasai and tell about Jesus. They listened with surprise and wondered how the man talking had managed to get inside the box, exactly as Lemayan had, long, long ago, on that first day he had heard of his Good Shepherd, on that day he had feared the Grannies were planning to cut off his leg. He laughed at the memory!

Kokoo produced a folding table and chair and put the little machine that would show the pictures on it. Ng'oto Ntoyie called Lemayan and a friend to hang, somehow, her white sheet on the church tree. They struggled. It wasn't straight and waved a bit in the wind, but it would do. As soon as it was dark they started.

The first filmstrip was of a man who had found a baby leopard and took it home for his children to play with. The chief kept coming to warn the foolish man that that leopard was dangerous.

'That leopard will grow,' the man was warned. 'He will kill you and your children. It is his nature to kill.' The man refused to heed the warning.

'I'll feed it only porridge. If it doesn't get a taste of blood, it won't harm us,' the stubborn man insisted.

At first the crowd laughed at the man with the leopard. Then they grew silent. Then they started calling out to the man shown on the billowing white cloth, 'Man! Listen to the chief. Let him kill the leopard!' When the full-grown leopard at last leapt on the man, there was much shaking of heads and murmurs from the audience.

'Just as the chief warned that man to let him kill the leopard, so God is warning us to allow Him to rescue us from our sins,' Ng'oto Ntoyie explained.

When the next filmstrip was shown, there was no laughing but quiet, thoughtful attention. They saw pictures of the arrest of Jesus, his trial, the carrying of the heavy cross, and then Jesus on the cross. There was a deep silence, with just some gasps of horror as they saw Jesus' suffering. Sankale came forward in the silence and explained to the crowd the purpose of the suffering and the response God wants from them. He challenged the listeners to accept the sacrifice Jesus had made for their sins. There was a breathless silence.

A man got up and came to stand next to Sankale. Lemayan saw it was his father. What was father going to say?

'You all know me,' he started. 'You know that my wife and my son follow this Jesus we have seen in these pictures. I thought, in my pride, that this new way was for our children, for school people. We have seen, in these preachers who have brought church to us, a newness, a joy and certainty that is good to see. It is something we did not get from our traditional way of honouring the great Enkai. Tonight I tell you all, from this day you will see me sitting here on these benches, even sitting with my children – singing with them, learning with them, until I too know that certainty and change in my own life that our preacher friends have found.' Lemayan's heart nearly burst with joy!

After that, two young men who had been very interested in the preaching and had followed the preachers all around to hear more, stood up in front, together. 'We have something to ask these grandmothers with white hair,' one said. 'We hear that you have times when men like us, who have never been to school, can go to your village and learn to read and know these words better. Do you have room for us in your school? When can we come?'

Ng'oto Ntoyie stepped forward, took a hand of each in her hands. 'Brothers, we here and now accept you as learners in our school. And if you are ready, you may come with us tonight. The next two-week course starts tomorrow.' The whole crowd erupted into applause, clapping and shouting 'Meisisi Enkai' (Praise God). They were excited to have their own people going to learn to be the leaders of their church, the church that had been born that morning.

It was time for the visitors to go. The vehicles soon filled up. Naado had two mothers and three children added to her load, as well as the Mamas who had come with her. The Land Cruiser had the

three evangelists, as well as the brand new pupils for the evangelists' school. Then they realised Lemayan was missing.

'Where is Lemayan?' Ng'oto Ntoyie called out. 'We are ready to go.' They heard a scuffle and voices in the dark approaching them.

Lemayan went up to the Land Rover window. 'Naado, do you have room for another passenger.'

'Yes, Lemayan,' Naado agreed. 'Where is he? We can squeeze one more in'

'Right here behind me!' said Lemayan, laughing. He pulled a reluctant goat into the beam of the vehicle's lights. 'Naado, I want to give

this goat as a present to you and the Mamas, to say thank you for all you and everyone there have done for me down through the years. I can now walk well. I have nearly finished High School, and best of all, I am now following and serving Jesus, all because of you and the Child Care Centre.'

Naado, embarrassed by the lovely gesture, thanked him and Lemayan and his goat filled the last bit of space in the Land Rover. As everyone else waved and shouted goodbye, Lemayan was silent. He could scarcely take in all that had happened on this, the very best and most wonderful day of his life.

Only two more terms at school! Exams to pass! Then what more wonderful surprises would his Good Shepherd have in store for him?

His Dreams for the Future

'How different are life at school and life at home!' was Lemayan's thought as he settled into school again. For four weeks he had been immersed in Maasai life.

But life was great back at school too. Class work was demanding but there was still much time for Christian activities. He was now the leader of the Bible Study that Kamau had taken him to when he was a frightened little Form 1 pupil.

He also did a lot of praying - he prayed much for his father, that he would really be changed and sure of his new faith. He prayed for those two young men learning to be preachers. He prayed earnestly that people would not lose interest in the church. That it would continue, Sunday by Sunday, to be a centre of witness and blessing.

But in that final term at High School he also prayed seriously about his future. That future, he hoped, would be shared with a beautiful young Maasai lady, Pilale, whom he had met at a Christian Union Leaders' Seminar. They had chatted easily at the first meal, when they sat together. They seemed to have so much in common, most importantly their living faith, that for the four days of the seminar, they spent their spare time in each other's company. He was so sure of his position in Christ's family that Lemayan found he had lost his fear of rejection. Pilale didn't even seem to notice his disability. By the time the seminar was over they had exchanged addresses, with promises, on both sides, to write often. They had important exams ahead and then years of training. She was aiming at nursing and he as yet, didn't know what his Good Shepherd had planned for him.

The last school holiday before his finals, he decided to go home for two weeks rest and contact with his family. The following two weeks he planned to go to the Child Care Centre and beg a place to study, to get ready for his final High School exams.

It was while at home that God clearly pointed the way for his future.

'Son, you have come home at the right time to help us,' his father greeted him eagerly. Then Lemayan found that he had arrived home to find everyone overflowing with exciting news.

'Since the time we started our church,' his father explained, 'our community has become very united and we are wanting to make many changes in our lifestyle. The big step we have taken is that, through the chief, we are applying for title deeds to this land that we live on, so that we can establish a Group Ranch. We hear that rich people are fast buying up the land because they understand legal and government ways. The Ministry of Lands has responded to us by sending a surveyor. He is at the chief's village right now. You, my son, have a good knowledge of the white man's tongue and how to fill in government forms. Come with me to the chief's village now. It is good that you went to school for all these years. You can help us now.'

'Father!' Lemayan cried out joyfully, 'that is wonderful news!' He rejoiced in this new idea with all his heart. His family and whole community establishing a ranch! Fencing, a borehole, earth-dams, a dip, good range management and pedigree bulls to upgrade the stock – all these dreams tumbled round in his mind.

'Yes, son,' his father replied. 'I am glad too. But let's hurry over to the chief's village. We don't want that surveyor to give up and go off home, just because he can't understand us!'

Arriving at the chief's village, they found a good number of the elders gathered. Lemayan was welcomed warmly. He was the answer to their predicament. They were finding their small knowledge of Kiswahili was not enough for understanding the surveyor and even more inadequate for expressing clearly all they were asking for.

So, young as he was, he took his seat between the chief and the surveyor, who could understand nothing of the language being talked all around him. Patiently Lemayan gave him the gist of the long speeches the elders were making. Later he felt uncomfortable standing up before his fathers and grandfathers, interpreting to them what the surveyor was saying in answer to their requests. The elders knew exactly what land they wanted. Having grazed their herds on these plains since childhood, they could explain very clearly, the land that should be included – they knew to the last hill, riverbed or rocky outcrop.

Early the next day Lemayan was an important member of the group who tramped the plains with the surveyor. He explained to the elders what the surveyor was doing with his mysterious instruments. He explained to the surveyor all the intricacies of the discussion of the elders. Was the boundary to be behind the hill or over the top? Was the far bank or the near bank of the sandy riverbed to be the boundary? He helped with the hammering in of the iron pegs and was asked to go to all the villages the next day to warn the women and children not to steal those markers – so ideal for digging holes for posts when building a new house!

Walking home with his father he shared what was in his heart.

'Father, in these past months I have been praying about what I will do next year. Now I know! I knew the moment I heard that the community is planning a 'group-ranch' here. Please may I go to a veterinary college? I will go and study hard so that I will be able to help you all to establish that modern ranch that you plan to develop. I will learn all about boreholes and earth dams, to have enough water for people and livestock, for growing fodder-crops and vitamin-giving vegetables for the families. I will learn all about dipping cattle and veterinary medicines so that it will be safe to have high-grade beef and dairy cattle. With the knowledge of proper range management our grasslands will improve, but we could also make hay and store it for the dry times that always come. I am already studying Animal Husbandry at school, but I would need far more training to make this proposed ranch a success.

Father's head was reeling with all this talk of strange ideas. But Lemayan dreamed on!

Once the community owned the land, they would build a school for the children. Lemayan thought longingly of his friend Kemendere – perhaps he would leave the school at Magadi where he was teaching, to come and run the school. They would also build a church. Perhaps Kemendere had already found a good Christian wife. She could be the teacher for a Nursery School that could use the church building during the week. His dreams rushed on to include using the school building, during the school holidays, for Christian conferences, literacy courses and training courses on good livestock management.

But most importantly, in all his dreams of the future, his lovely friend, Pilale, was there beside him. She could run a clinic for the local people and have a community health programme to improve the general health in the villages. But above all, in his dream, she was his wife. Perhaps caring for their home and children and being his wife, would keep her too busy. Then they would need a second nurse!

But, sighed Lemayan to himself, 'I still have to pass my High School final exams. I still have years of college ahead. Pilale has her years of nursing training to get through too. But all this is in the good hands of my Saviour Jesus, my Friend and Good Shepherd.'

Lemayan lifted up his heart in thanks to God.

'Thank you God for sending your Son, Jesus. Thank you for your gift of cattle, but your gifts of salvation and eternal life are much, much greater.'

'Thank you, Father, for also giving us your wonderful book so that we can know you and how to follow you.' Lemayan rejoiced that the Maasai, at last, had that whole Bible in their own mother tongue, to feed themselves from its riches.

'Thank you, my Good Shepherd, for giving me the chance of a good education that has opened my mind and will also equip me to come back to help my people.' Then he thanked God for all those who had guided him along the way to come to Jesus and to walk with Him – the Mamas, Naado and the Grannies, Kemendere, Kamau and also the evangelists who had helped the whole community. Truly he was Lemayan – the blessed one.

At last his two worlds - home and school, Christianity and Maasai traditions, the old and the new - were coming together. By throwing out the bad and keeping the good, by rejecting the false and embracing the true – all could be one through

His Dreams for the Future

Jesus, Enkai's Son who has broken down the walls that divide.

Lemayan pulled himself back from his dreaming. Unless he hurried on to the Child Care Centre to do some revision and study for his coming exams, these dreams would never be a reality.

So he travelled eagerly on, into his future, into his dreams, in the safe loving care of his Good Shepherd.

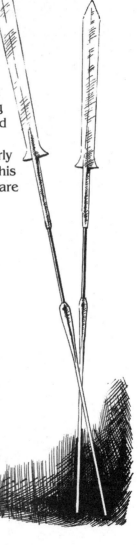

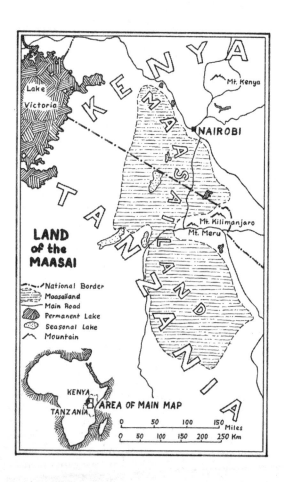

KENYA

Lake
Victoria

Mt. Kenya

NAIROBI

TANZANIA

Mt. Kilimanjaro
Mt. Meru

LAND
of the
MAASAI

National Border
Maasailand
Main Road
Permanent Lake
Seasonal Lake
Mountain

KENYA
TANZANIA

AREA OF MAIN MAP

0   50   100   150
                          Miles
0   50   100 150 200 250 Km

Who are The Maasai?

THE MAASAI – Then and Now.

The Maasai are a proud cattle people who live in the south of Kenya and across the border into Tanzania, where the great Game Parks are. The Maasai consider the game to be God's cattle and so they can live at peace with wild animals, in gratitude for giving them, the Maasai, all the cattle in the world. But lions are the exception! Every young warrior must have taken part in a successful lion hunt to be considered a man. Being so proud of their own culture they have not hungered after western ways and education like other Africans have. They believe in a Creator God who loves them (only) They don't worship ancestors like most Africans do because they don't believe there is life after death. They always enjoy hearing of heaven, of God sending his Son to be their "olkipoket" – sin-offering but many don't want to believe because many changes in behaviour would have to be made if they truly came to Jesus.

But these days there are many Maasai Christians. The educated ones go to churches like ours, as they are part of modern Kenya. Those who are still part of the cattle-village life, worship in meeting places in the shade of a tree, or in a little corrugated-iron building. They sing songs in their own kind of music, with clapping and dancing, songs that they make up as they praise the God they know in truth in Jesus. The educated Maasai have changed, either in jobs or professions, or have ranches with beef cattle and are prosperous, except when drought devastates all cattle people. Others carry on their old ways except where government pressures squeeze them to conform.

Africa Inland Mission

AIM was founded over 100 years ago when the young Peter Cameron Scott, a man with a clear vision, gathered around him a group of fellow workers. Cameron Scott records that he "...seemed to see a line of mission stations stretching from the coast, on into the mysteries of the Sahara Desert."

The small group that arrived in Mombasa in 1895 made their way inland. It was not long before disease overtook them and before two years were up, all but one of them had died. Scott himself died of blackwater fever. But all was not lost. The survivor stayed on and before long others joined him. Over the years the work has spread, initially from Kenya out to Tanzania, Congo, Uganda and Central Africa Republic. Just as all these countries have found political independence, so the churches planted by AIM have taken on their independence, so that AIM's role is now largely that of a support to these churches.

As well as throughout Africa AIM also works among Africans in the United States, UK and Romania. AIM currently has 750 members from 15 or so different nationalities, most of whom are working in Africa.

In all new endeavours we are looking for partnership with national churches and other mission agencies developing leadership in all sectors of African life. We are presently researching new openings in parts of Africa where we have not previously worked. Alongside those involved directly in these ministries we also have administrators, accountants, pilots and aircraft mechanics, and teachers for the children of missionaries.

Contact details: Africa Inland Mission, 3 Halifax Place, Nottingham NG1 1QN.
www.aim-eur.org

About the Author...

"Lorna Eglin, born in Cape Town, South Africa, was a missionary with AIM International in Kenya for 45 years. She, together with her missionary colleague, Betty Allcock, are happily retired in South Africa. They are still in touch with many Kenya friends and are pushing 'missions' in their local church. Lorna is still writing - currently about the adventures they had as they worked with the proud cattle-people, the Maasai and other Maasai-speaking groups."

Pray for Africa and The Maasai

Remarkable changes have taken place in Africa over the past thirty years, but there are underlying concerns. Patrick Johnstone in Operation World outlines five trends to watch. For us, these are matters for prayer.

- **AIDS** continues to place a heavy toll on the continent. Weak governmentscivil unrest and war should motivate us to pray for Christian leaders in all areas of government and society.

- **Tension** between Christian and Muslim populations is particularly evident along the 'line' which extends from Senegal across the Sahel to Ethiopia. This sometimes erupts in violence as seen in Nigeria.

- **Poverty.** Africa's share of world trade is decreasing, its people are becoming poorer and trained professionals are not staying to practise in their native countries. Some debt relief has been agreed but many counties are still burdened by debt repayment.

- **Traditions.** Despite enormous growth in the church traditional African religions still command wide influence. It may not be possible to fully understand Africa's problems without taking this into account.

- **Maasai Children.** That the many Maasai children, and the millions of children throughout Africa, will come to know Jesus as their Saviour while they are young. That they will change to become new people inside, not just change to western ways and clothes.

- **Education.** That Maasai children, and the many others, who want education, choice of careers and marriage partners, may have the opportunity and will use their freedom wisely.
- **Abuse.** Maasai children are usually loved and valued, but many children in Africa are abused, abandoned and exploited. Pray for protection by loving adults of all children.
- **Orphans.** That Africa's children who are being orphaned and are suffering through aids and war will receive the home-care, health-care and the love they should have.
- **Missionaries.** That God would bless the missionaries and aid organizations with safety and all they need to help Africa's children. That help will reach the really needy, that none will be left out.
- **Me and You.** That God would show each of us who read this what our part could be in helping Africa's vulnerable children, in prayer, giving and sending help - and even going ourselves.

A Girl of Two Worlds

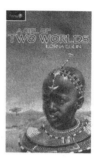

By Lorna Eglin

Nosim is ordered to attend the missionary boarding school. The chief thinks that having a Maasai in the school will make them important. Thus begins Nosim's double life where she juggles the world of school and Christianity with Maasai life. At first it appears both lifestyles cannot co-exist. Nosim eventually realises that if you don't give your life to Jesus completely you are not following him at all. But does becoming a Christian mean leaving family and culture and identity behind? The perfect ending to this story is how Nosim is encouraged to take the gospel to her own people, by remaining a Maasai woman and a Christian. She is in actual fact a girl of two worlds – definitely a Christian and definitely Maasai.

ISBN 1 85792 8393

African Adventures

By Dick Anderson

Incredible stories from the missionary frontier in Africa.

Read about Lions, Hyenas, Crocodiles and Snakes as well as the human beings who live and work alongside these dangerous animals.

Laugh and Shudder in the African Savannah.

Adventure is only a page away.

ISBN: 1-85792-8075

CHRISTIAN FOCUS

Good Books with the Real Message of Hope

Staying faithful – Reaching out!

Christian Focus Publications publishes books for adults and children under its three main imprints: Christian Focus, Mentor and Christian Heritage. Our books reflect that God's word is reliable and Jesus is the way to know him, and live forever with him.

Our children's publication list includes a Sunday school curriculum that covers pre-school to early teens; puzzle and activity books. We also publish personal and family devotional titles, biographies and inspirational stories that children will love.

If you are looking for quality Bible teaching for children then we have an excellent range of Bible story and age specific theological books.

From pre-school to teenage fiction, we have it covered!

Find us at our web page: www. christianfocus.com